Φ

THE PHILOSOPHIAN RECORD

A STARFARER'S TRUE NAME

E.B. KINDER

ILLUMIFY
MEDIA.COM

Contents

CHAPTER 1

Megalodon

Mia woke with a start and slid her form into the corner of her cell. It was cold beneath her, suggesting she'd only just been put back in.

"What have they done to me this time?" she said to herself.

"Mostly tests, from what I saw," said the voice from the other side of the vent above her. It was a familiar voice she had come to trust, though she still wasn't sure who it belonged to. It was a deep voice, robust and commanding, yet gentle, and she felt reassured to hear him.

Since she'd arrived at the black labs of *Megalodon*, she'd undergone multiple biografts and genetic therapies in short succession. The contract had been for *one* biograft, and the whole experiment was to see if the new gene-splicing process could give her a natural and instinctive use of her new cat ears. A run of bad luck had put her in a tight scrape financially, and of the projects she'd been offered to "volunteer" for to pay off her debts, this one had been the most appealing. She vaguely remembered even liking the idea at one point, although now her memory was so hazy she might as well have chalked it up as a dream.

That had been before one of the ship's crime lords had spotted her in her cell and seen her biografts. He'd observed her reactions. The natural twitch of her ears had particularly impressed him, enough so to bribe the scientists into seeing how much further they could take her transformation. It was a blatant breach of contract, but she was in no position to stop them from inside her cell. The nomadic megaships weren't known for investigating these matters thoroughly, if at all. In fact, their "alternative law enforcement" moderator squads were picked less for their interest in protecting the innocent and more for their skill in keeping peace on the ship for those in command. She had no family left aboard, and inquiring about a missing person risked unwanted attention. The moderators were good at making such inquiries bad for one's future.

She had fought the physicians as much as she could, but all that changed was their protocol. Now when they operated or worked on her, they put her under or strapped her down. She was remembering less and less of her past now, and while her senses seemed plenty sharp, her mind was in a fog from the constant injections, and she feared she had lost some of her ability to reason. Even her name seemed off, like an abbreviation or proxy of her born name. It made her sick just thinking about it.

"Are your nail beds healing well, m'lady?" the voice asked.

"More or less," she muttered, looking down at her fingers. The wounds had closed, and her nail beds still looked human, but she could only guess if they'd ever be the same. They had been part of the last effort to modify her to their so-called client's liking, and it hadn't gone well. Indeed, the operation had been closer to an exercise in torture than science, and she didn't want to think about what they wanted to do with her when they were finished—that is, if they ever did finish.

"How about you, Tyber? Are you holding up all right?" she asked the voice from the vent.

"I'm still watching the way these men work, and I'm pleased to say I'm regaining my strength. In fact, I think I feel strong enough now."

"Strong enough for what?" she asked.

"Never mind," he said. "Just focus on resting, m'lady."

Mia decided to follow that instruction. She was tired, and the lab wasn't going to get any quieter than it was now, since the staff seemed to be rotating for a new shift. Hopefully, she would get a little rest this time.

When she woke, there was a face at the door. It was chimeric green and different from the ones she'd seen before, hosting what looked to be scales. A lab technician's face appeared alongside it, and as the door opened, she could see the scaled figure step back.

"You're right, boss, you can see the difference," said the scaly one. "I'm a little jealous. Even my features don't move that naturally, and I got these as a kid."

"Come on out," ordered the lab technician.

Mia hesitated, and an instant later two more men came in to drag her out. She recognized the faces of the lead scientist and of the crime lord who had bribed the staff. The latter smiled profanely and reached up to grip her chin, which prompted Mia to withdraw from him. She would have bit him if she'd thought to.

"We're concerned about the claw biografts you specified. Initial tests show they may not produce the desired outcome, but if you like, we're willing to attempt it again," said the scientist matter-of-factly.

"A declawed kitten is still marketable, and I'm eager to see the reception this one gets in the rouge district," said the crime lord.

Even if Mia hadn't known what he meant, his surly grin and the look of veiled distaste on the chimeric one's face as he looked away told her more than enough. She cried out, and this time she did bite the man holding her right arm and struggled to pry herself free from the man gripping her left.

"You two, hold her still," said the lead scientist as he prepared a syringe.

"Perhaps some conditioning is in order," said the crime lord. "I know a man who—"

A crash on the far side of the lab cut the man's statement short. Mia managed to turn just far enough to spot an enormous white tiger from the corner of her eye. It charged toward them in a frenzy. In an instant it tackled the scientist, crushing bones with its sheer weight, letting forth a stunning roar that shook her to the core, its sheer power rattling her in her own skin. In another instant, it grabbed a lab technician by the throat and swung the man about like a rag doll. Everyone scattered, and Mia fell backward as she scrambled away in horror. When the lifeless body was sufficiently broken, the tiger tossed it aside dismissively before turning to approach her. Then to her astonishment, it looked her in the eye and said, "Are you uninjured, m'lady?"

"T-Tyber?" she gasped.

"On my back! Quickly!" he said.

Too astonished to question, Mia obeyed and gripped the tiger by the scruff of the neck as he sped forward. As they approached the outer corridors, the tiger angled right and then left again at the bend, and searched about wildly for an exit as they entered a large room filled with test equipment.

"Straight ahead!" cried Mia, pointing.

Tyber understood, and leaped over the metal cabinet before them. There, on the far side of the lab, was the door leading out. Upon seeing this exit, he barreled toward it, knocking workers, crates, and bins aside. They whipped past the security checkpoint before the guard even had time to fall out of his chair. They then fled into the halls she'd entered by. An alarm had begun to ring as they fled, but its sound was already dim. Mia navigated Tyber through the labyrinth of unadorned maintenance corridors and storerooms, leaving the sterile confines of the lab behind them.

"So the whole time you were a tiger?" asked Mia, trying to take in what was happening.

"You're surprised? I thought you'd seen me enough times in the adjoining pen to know."

"I hadn't seen you speaking then!" interjected Mia.

"I learned from listening when they tried to teach me commands . . . and when I was talking to you," he said.

"You're a quick study," said Mia, marveling at his ability.

"Thank you. To be fair, though, you did most of the talking."

Mia quickly learned Tyber had the strength to jump almost anywhere in the chambers, and so long as they were quiet when perched in the pipes, catwalks, or immense vents and trays of wires that dominated the overhead space, they were generally able to go unseen. A careless footfall onto one of the large vents very nearly revealed them, but Tyber's predatory instincts prevented their discovery, for he pounced on the guard before an alarm could be raised. However, this still caused Mia to slip and bruise a shoulder as she fell from her perch and into a pile of pallets and cardboard scraps. Her shirt torn, but otherwise mostly uninjured, she resolved to simply run alongside Tyber from that point on. For what felt like hours, theirs continued to be a nerve-racking game of hide-and-seek as guards searched the nearby chambers.

"So why didn't you say something when I was out? You know, when I *could* see you," whispered Mia as they matched stride once again.

"I wouldn't deign to speak to *them*," said Tyber bitterly. "I preferred our conversation to theirs, so I thought I'd keep it our secret. Now, how far until we are out?"

Mia sputtered. She'd never thought about what she would do if she ever *escaped* the lab. The idea had sounded too wild. She racked her brain to think of what they might have to do next, but to little result. The labs were moving quickly to contain them, and they were closing up the escapes faster than she could think of them. Even as she led Tyber through the halls, her mind seized up, until she slowed her pace, coming to a stop before yet another sealed door.

"I-I don't think we can."

"I don't understand," said Tyber. "I may have been young when I was brought here, but I've seen enough of the outside world to know there has to be an exit to this place. There is more to the world than this steel hive, and we are now committed to returning to it."

"I like how you think, Tyber," said Mia and hugged the gentle beast closely. "But we're in space. Outside of this ship is miles upon miles of open nothingness neither of us could survive in, not even for a moment. We would need a vessel to cross it in order to reach a planet. That is what separates us from the 'outside' that you want to see."

Tyber stared for a long while, glancing about before asking, "You're sure about this?"

Mia nodded. The light from the sealed door's narrow-slit window cast a dim outline on the floor. Through it, a combination of signs and neon lights from the adjoining market sector of the ship could barely be glimpsed beyond, teasing them with their proximity. Mia felt like a tired child and desperately wished her clouded head would clear so she could think of a better way out, even as she tried to fight back her despair.

"I don't understand—if this is true, can we not obtain one of these vessels?" asked Tyber at length.

Mia sighed. "We can't steal one; I wouldn't know how to run it if we did. Even if I somehow found someone willing to transport a girl *and* a tiger, I would need money to hitch a ride, and I don't have a crypto to my name right now. I was hoping we could find the authorities after we got out of here, but they've closed the bulkheads off already. This closed door tells me our sector was sealed off the moment they sounded the alarm. Any open exits will have heavily armed guards and hired guns by now. They'll find us soon enough, and then we'll be back where we began."

"I see," said Tyber in a tone of resignation. "I'm sorry, m'lady."

"Don't feel sad for me, Tyber. This is the happiest I've been in months," said Mia, tearing up. "I just . . . wish I could stay with you . . . a while . . . longer."

Mia began to weep into Tyber's long fur. Tyber sat close, his head on her shoulder, and they waited.

Neither moved to look up as footsteps approached. However, the female voice that spoke did not say what she expected.

"Hey, are you all right?" the woman's voice asked. Her tone was consoling and gentle, even upbeat.

Mia looked up and wiped away her tears. The stranger was not part of the lab. Rather, she was dressed in casual garb. With her violet hair and a black jacket, she looked like a denizen of the ship, although she seemed inordinately clean for one. She was also wearing a subtle perfume that boasted uncharacteristic elegance for a space nomad. In fact, according to Mia's nose, this woman didn't seem like a citizen of *Megalodon* at all. Tyber watched intently as Mia stared up at the woman, who knelt over her with a soft smile and a look of concern.

At length, she reached out a hand to Mia. Tyber responded with a warning growl.

"Easy, big fella. I don't want to hurt you. Is this your friend?" asked the stranger.

Mia nodded reticently. The fact she was asking who they were indicated she didn't know where they came from or why they were there, but she was still unsure who this person was or whether she could be trusted. Her staunch lack of fear was spellbinding, and the question remained: What was she doing here if she wasn't part of the lab?

"I'm Electra. What's your name?"

"M-Mia," she replied, then capped her hands over her mouth in horror as the sound she made sounded like a cat's meow.

"Is there anything they *haven't* done to me yet!" she said in an outburst of rage.

Electra laughed. "Well, I guess it's good to hear you speak. It's nice to meet you, Mia. Come on, let's get you two out of this place."

"Why are you helping me?" asked Mia, shrinking back.

"Because that's how she is," said a second voice from some distance down the hall to their left. They spied a figure gliding toward them. She was so small she looked like a child.

"I warned you this would happen if we came to *Megalodon* again. We can't help everybody, Electra," said the child.

"I don't want to help everyone. Just these two," said Electra brightly.

"But why?" asked Mia again.

"You don't need a reason to help someone! Helping others is one of life's greatest joys!" exclaimed Electra, then said in a quieter tone, "The truth is, I overheard you two talking earlier. I gathered from it that you're both escapees from the lab. I may not know how you ended up here, but I'm all too aware what a shady bunch the guys who run these labs are, and as such I couldn't be happier to get you away from them."

Mia's hair had felt like it would stand on end as Electra commented about overhearing Tyber talking to her. She briefly panicked a glance at Tyber, who seemed less agitated, but calmly asked, "How do you intend to do that?"

By now they could all hear the distant noises of searching guards and the sounds of armsuits, a type of power-actuated combat armor. Layered with strong plates over arrays of servos and synthetic muscle fibers, armsuits were carefully designed to augment the soldier's strength, mobility, and, of course, durability.

It signaled the black lab staff had brought in specialized weaponry to capture them.

"First things first, we need to put distance between them and us. That demands a distraction that can allow us to breach the bulkheads without alerting *Megalodon's* command systems," said the child. She sounded like she was presenting an agenda for a tea party, not preparing to fight off a group of heavily armed guards.

"Aster's right," said Electra. "Now, correct me if I'm wrong, but you would be pleased to see that lab destroyed, right?"

Mia and Tyber nodded emphatically, and Aster placed her hand on the wall and said, "Done."

A moment later they heard several new alarms. At least two arc flashes could be seen down the far end of the corridor. The fire suppression systems burst to life as lights exploded and half a dozen cables and pipes broke free of their placements.

"A bit theatrical, but a little steam and sparks to screen a withdrawal never hurt," said Aster placidly, resting her hand over her heart.

Mia stared at the child in horror, trying to guess how she had done it. She'd heard of hackers creating that kind of havoc before. Usually they needed at least half an hour and oodles of gear to make something like that happen, but Aster had created the same result in an instant like it was a parlor trick.

"How . . . how did you—"

"Less talking, more running. Aster's diversion won't distract the guards long; the aim was to confuse the internal sensors," said Electra as she led them down the hall Aster had arrived from.

"I take it you plan to have Donnerschlag cut us a return path to the docking ports?" asked Aster in a "pass the cream" tone that belied the situation.

"Something like that," said Electra. "It's on its way now."

"Donner-what?" asked Mia, still trying to stay apace of the situation as it was unfolding.

"Our ride. You don't have any problem with riding automated mechs or flyers, do you?" asked Electra.

Gunfire sounded, suggesting someone had spotted them, but little could be said for certain in the confused din of noises caused by the disrupted systems. They turned the corner to see something cutting through the wall ahead. The bulkhead fell away to reveal a large machine that folded and turned to provide a platform for them to mount and hovered in place in the chasmal shaft it appeared from.

"Right on time, Donner," said Electra. "Everyone aboard!"

Once on, they began to descend the shaft. A quiet settled, and for a time Mia simply listened to the other two women and looked about, questioning her surroundings as she observed the sheer space of the shaft. She made a passive but heartfelt attempt to comfort Tyber, who crouched as close to the center of the flying contraption as he could, unamused by the height.

"Well, so much for going in and out quietly," said Electra. Turning to Aster, she asked, "Did you get to reprogram that rogue AI while you were here?"

"It's their main computer, and no, I didn't reprogram it. To reprogram it would be to change what it's doing. Our coming was, in part, to confirm it's doing exactly what we prescribed and nothing else. We had a nice conversation, and I gave it some added contingency plans if the command staff got suspicious," said Aster with an aloof huff. "According to Invictus, the whole ship is in an uproar, and everyone in the sector is being detained. The good news is we won't have to move as cautiously since the surveillance is quite thoroughly compromised, but the docks are on a temporary lockdown. We will have to enter the *Anawim* via space walk."

"Well, that's a problem," said Electra. "You and I could get there, and in theory we could nab Mia a space suit . . ." Electra trailed off as she looked at Tyber.

"I wouldn't suggest it," said Aster. "Nomad space suits are notorious for being hard to operate due to their varied clientele, and are often modified by their owners to kill other operators in order to discourage theft. I suggest we find another option for both of them."

"They what?" exclaimed Electra. "Why would someone want to booby-trap their own space suit? That's so spiteful!"

"How about a sealed cargo pod?" said Mia suddenly.

"Cargo pod?" asked Tyber.

"It's a small box that can seal itself tightly enough to keep pressure in space," said Mia. "It would be cramped, and we would have only a few minutes before we ran out of oxygen, but if it isn't a long trip, we could do it. After all, we'll be weightless outside the airlock."

"Let's find a suitable crate first," Aster suggested. "Besides, we still have a ways to go, and a better alternative might present itself."

Donnerschlag deposited them on a platform beyond a damaged panel, then promptly vanished as the ten foot tall transforming robot drone engaged an optical camouflage.

Darkness dominated the hall, forcing Mia to hold Aster's hand, and she felt comforted as Tyber brushed close to her in the low visibility. Lights snapped on, and a group of armed troops blocked their path. Mia's heart sank when she saw their long robes and hoods covering their polished, expressionless red face masks and armored vests. They weren't moderators like she'd hoped, but members of one of *Megalodon's* cults, possibly the Adherance, who were known for their fanatic mannerisms and chilling treatment of outsiders in their territory.

"Hands high, all of you!" said the leader of the group. "Command, we have the Baihu specimen, accompanied by—" The leader cut himself short as his eyes settled on Electra and cried, "No! It's you!"

The lights flickered. Two troops flinched and directed their rifles across the group nervously.

"Command? Come in, Command! We have a situation!" yelled one as they looked about. As the lights darkened, two of the four guards had vanished, accompanied by a thud on the far wall. The remaining soldiers engaged flashlights to offset the dimmed surroundings, but to no avail, and Mia's ears detected a whipping sound like a wire or a rope winding up to snap. All at once, the masked cult members had their rifles wrenched from them, and two more thuds followed. The lights stopped their flickering as if queued that the fight was over, and Electra tossed aside the rifle of the last (now limp) cultist.

"Nice timing with the comms and lights, Aster," said Electra.

"I know you," muttered the lead soldier as he staggered to get up again. "Your appearance is different, but I've seen that technique before. You're the one who killed them!"

"Do I know you, mister?" asked Electra, put off by the cultist's tone.

"Forgetting won't absolve you! You may have given your memories to the white demon, Philos, but it doesn't make you any less responsible!"

With that he reached for a hidden pistol from beneath the folds of cloth, but before it had even cleared the holster, Electra had closed the distance with him and landed an uppercut that crumpled his steel mask and sent the cultist sprawling. Mia froze for a moment, and even Tyber was awestruck by the speed at which she had maneuvered. With the ambush thwarted, they kept moving and soon passed a corner where a lad who had clearly been within earshot looked up but tried as hard as he could not to draw attention to himself. Electra set a crypto chip near him and, with her finger over her mouth, gave him a charming wink and said, "We were never here, okay?"

They made their way to a loading floor just outside the external docks of the ship. Mia spotted an empty cargo pod about the size of a large trunk. Electra followed her gaze and eyed it dubiously as they approached, then objected outright when Mia began climbing in.

"Now, hold on! I admit it's not a bad idea. I could walk you across the catwalk in under a minute. However, you're going to be trapped there once we lock you in. Are you sure you'll be all right in a space that small?"

"We could at least find separate containers so you have a little more space," said Aster.

"I hesitated when we got out of the lab and they boxed Tyber and me in," said Mia, trying to control her breathing and swallow as she fought to stifle her rising sense of panic. "I-I'm counting on you two. I don't know either of you well, but I think I'd rather get put in a trunk by you two than in another cell by *Megalodon*'s moderators. I've lived here long enough to know they're even more bribable than the lab staff."

Electra smiled softly and heaved the cargo pod to the airlock before she helped the two in.

"I won't let you down," she reassured them as she latched the box shut. The cramped space was dark, save for a small viewing panel intended for workers to preview the box's contents. It now served as their only view out. They could feel the box being gently shifted and the sounds outside fading as the airlock decompressed.

CHAPTER 2

Electra and Asterope

"I don't like this," said Tyber, fighting to retain his composure.

Mia tried to endure the tiger's panting as he pawed the wall of the box and endeavored to help him stay calm, but she could tell he was growing panicky.

"Just keep looking at the view outside. I picked this one just so we'd have a panel to look through. We'll be out in just a moment. You'll see," said Mia, though she knew all too well how completely false her statement was.

When the airlock opened, the artificial gravity disengaged, and Tyber flexed until he became rigid, bracing himself against the inside of the small box in response to his sudden weightlessness. Mia feared he was going to deform the box and compromise the seal of the pod. They watched closely as their view spun in space, and Mia did a double take as she realized Electra, who was pushing them along, wasn't wearing a space suit. Not even a helmet!

Her heart sank as she remembered the words of the cultist from earlier. Of the few powers that could give a person a body that could endure the vacuum of space, Philos and its AI, Philosophia sprang to mind, and she realized she was indeed trusting her fate to outsiders loyal to another power entirely. However, she didn't have time to ponder this thoroughly, as she heard Tyber make an unsettling sound.

"Mia, I don't feel—"

"No! Don't even think about puking in here!" Mia shouted, clamping his mouth shut. Tyber twitched with nausea, reeling in the confined space, smashing Mia against the inside of the box. Mia's head throbbed with pain, overridden only by her abject fear of the unspeakable mess she would endure if she unclasped her arms around Tyber's jaw.

"Please! Just a little longer! If you throw up in here—"

However, these pleas proved a vain gesture.

When Electra opened the pod in their ship, the *Anawim*, she was met by a stench that nearly made her gag.

"I hate my life," said Mia dejectedly as she lay limp in the pod, covered in vomit.

Aster pinched her nose and gently replied, "I'll get a damp cloth. Why don't you shed those clothes, and Electra can take you and Tyber to our refresher. Can I ask you to wash Tyber down, too, or would you prefer one of us do that?"

Mia had no objections to washing the big cat and followed Electra to the refresher. It was compact like any ship facility, making it another cramped operation, but she sighed with wonder and relief when she realized it wasn't a droplet deposition system for sponging away grime like she'd used on *Megalodon*, but a proper *shower*!

She could have fallen asleep in that heavenly stream of hot water, and Tyber didn't mind its warmth either, but she had no idea how long such a system could work and didn't feel right exhausting the ship's resources for herself (although she did feel justified in basking for just a moment). She used the handheld showerhead in short bursts, soaping herself and Tyber down. When she emerged, she found herself staring quite hard at the face that stared back in the mirror. Until now, she had only had distorted glimpses of herself in the metallic paneling and faint reflections in glass windows when the lighting was right. Her biografted appearance had become a matter of suspense, and now that she saw her true reflection, she wasn't sure what to make of it. Her hair had always been a bit on the dark side, but now it had a sector near the ear fluff that must have hybridized after the graft, because patches around it had browned or bleached blond, if not white. It was not unlike the patches on a calico cat and probably came as a result or byproduct of the genetic splicing, and as she brushed her hair back into a kempt state, she found she had to admit, her ears matched the arrangement well. As for the ears themselves, she only needed a glance to see how the movement had caught the crime lord's attention. They moved freely, like an expression of her face, dictating her mood and attention such that it almost took more conscious effort to keep them still than let them act to their calling. To her relief, her face was still very human, and her pupils had not been made into slits, which actually puzzled her, as she vividly remembered them doing *something* to her eyes. In a sense it was the ideal outcome, yet seeing it now brought her surprisingly little relief.

When they were clean, she toweled herself off and set to blow-drying Tyber. The tiger basked in the warm breeze, preferring the drying process over the cleaning itself. When she finished, Mia emerged to see Aster holding a simple change of clothes that looked by their sizing to have been Electra's.

"Electra wants to know if you were attached to your old outfit in any way," she asked as she discreetly looked away and presented the garments.

"Not really," said Mia.

"Oh good, because I spaced them," said Electra from down the hall. "I'll replace them with whatever you want, but that crate was rank!"

"I can imagine," said Mia, distracted upon seeing that Electra had changed clothes as well as appearance. Her hair was now a beautiful chestnut-brown, which draped across her back in long beautiful locks befitting the scent she'd detected when they first met. She looked gentler, more elegant, and yet no less indomitable. Aster's appearance and attire had similarly changed, and Mia could see why they had not chosen these looks for *Megalodon*, as the contrast was akin to a swan shedding a disguise of peacock feathers. As she followed them to the bridge, she managed to ask, "Where are we now?"

"We're parked about fifty kilometers from the mega-ship's main structure. Come and see for yourself," said Electra.

They looked out to see the mammoth ship in orbit, its escorts moving like insects near its titanic frame. Yet it was Tyber who seemed most intrigued, for he almost climbed onto the console as he stared into the depths.

"Mia," Tyber asked, "is that the iron hive we fled?"

"That's it. That's *Megalodon*, the city-ship without borders."

"And the night sky around it. Is that the vast space between that you spoke of?"

Mia affirmed him again. This quizzing went on for some time, and Tyber picked his words carefully, sometimes pausing for some time between his questions. For a creature who had never seen these things to grasp them, he learned at an excellent pace. Mia enjoyed answering her friend, but at the same time she found herself getting drowsy and soon draped herself over her furry inquisitor. Before she knew it, she was fast asleep.

It was her ears that woke her again, and she inwardly chided herself for simply letting herself collapse like that so suddenly. She was dismayed how exhausted she felt and tried to feign sleep as she listened, giving herself a pinch to avoid drifting back off to sleep, then cracked a wandering eye open to look about. She'd been moved to a couch of sorts near the back of the bridge, likely intended for lounging, based on the layout, when she heard her name spoken. Tyber had not left her side, and he stirred when he realized she was awake. However, it was the discussion taking place that had her interest. Electra and Aster seemed to be transmitting to a third party.

"Look! Just because you found out she was there to pay off a debt doesn't mean she agreed to what they did to her!"

"I agree. From what I've put together, she went through an ordeal no one should have to," said the other voice.

"Then why are you being so evasive?" demanded Electra. "Are you going to help them or not?"

"I want to help her as much as you do, Electra. It's lack of information and limited options that constrain me. Consider this from a resources perspective. Your fiasco has already hit *Megalodon's* dark web and the Philos Network, and my assistant has been giving me dirty glances ever since I asked her to start covering your tracks. Now you want me to take on two nomad stowaways you've brought back with you."

"What about it? You aren't going to just abandon them, are you?" challenged Electra.

"That all depends on her, don't you think?" said the other voice. "I need time to ponder our options. I'll even consult Philosophia directly if you'd like, but I'm not omnipotent, so I can't promise anything. Meet me at the transfer point as we agreed. We'll discuss it then."

The man was dressed in white, and Mia spotted the insignia of Philos on his suit collar. This, and the last phrase he'd used, did not sit well with Mia, as "transfer point" implied goods for exchange. Standing, she crept toward the others.

"Well, I guess we better set a course," said Electra.

"Lay in a course, Invictus. Prepare to engage the slip drive," said Aster.

"Turn us around. Change course," said Mia impulsively.

"Mia, what's the matter?" asked Electra. "Where is it you're wanting to go?"

"A-Anywhere but where we're going," she said shakily.

"You're still half asleep, aren't you?" said Electra with a chuckle, but this chuckle was cut short when Mia drew the handgun from Electra's holster and pointed it at her head. Electra stared soberly without even a flinch, like the situation was still under control.

"M'lady, don't be rash," said Tyber. "We both know how formidable the two of them are."

"The man in that transmission was with Philos. I could see his insignia," insisted Mia. "That's who you work for, isn't it? Only cyborgs or androids could spacewalk without a suit. Does that mean Aster is an a-a-ndroid of some sort? That would explain her talent for hacking."

"Calm down, Mia," said Electra. "Put the gun away, that's not what anybody needs."

"Answer me then!" she demanded.

Electra paused and said solemnly, "Yes, we're cyborg augments. Posthumans, I believe the trending term is . . . and yes, we were doing work with Philos at the time we met you."

"Wait, Invictus," Aster suddenly commanded. A sound behind Mia indicated something active had shut down, and she glanced back to see a deploying turret retract into the roof again. Tyber crouched uneasily and gave a dull growl.

Aster spoke slowly, in a way that seemed to make the room itself grow cold as she did. It was almost a monotone.

"Mia, Electra and I want to help you right now, but I won't let you betray our trust and threaten my—"

"Aster, no. Let me handle this," interjected Electra. "Mia, I know you're scared. That you don't know who to trust and that you're worried someone will hurt you again. But I'm begging you: Please trust us a little longer. We're headed somewhere safe. It's true, Xenos works for Philos, but he's also a friend who can help you like few others can. Think about it, Mia. Even if Aster laid in a new course for you, where would you go?"

Mia stammered, letting the gun down, "I'm sorry. I'm just . . . I mean, I can't . . ."

"I know. I would be scared too," said Electra. "Hard as it is to imagine, I've been through something a little like this myself."

"An escaped experiment?" asked Mia confusedly.

"Well, not quite that," said Electra with an awkward laugh, "but I remember a time when I didn't know who to trust. That can happen when you lose your memory, after all."

"You what?" asked Mia in horror. She remembered the words of the Adherence cultist from before.

"It's true. I woke up one morning not knowing who I was or why I was there, save for a handful of flashbacks. I could barely remember my own name, let alone how I'd arrived there. I had to experience getting to know Aster and a few others all over again. I still regret that I nearly hurt Aster when I first woke. That I couldn't tell if she was a friend or an enemy. In the end, I had to let myself trust her before I could move forward at all."

Mia pondered Electra's story, then lowered the handgun. She then reached out and gripped Electra tightly as she sobbed. For a time, she stayed buried in Electra's arms, feeling Electra's hair as she in turn stroked Mia's soothingly.

"I'm sorry," blurted Mia after a time, "I just . . . Can you promise me you aren't going to hand me over to Philos?"

"Pinky promise!" said Electra gently.

Mia's mind, though clearer now, was still awash with many foreboding trains of thought. Philos was a corporate body with far-reaching influence that came courtesy of a powerful AI, dubbed "Philosophia" (or "Sophia," as some informally called it). Many colonies relied upon it to handle all manner of logistical affairs. Indeed, it comprised the majority of the data network infrastructure in the sector, if not the whole of colonized space, and much of the communication that happened anywhere went through it at one level or another.

Already its home nation of Altaire retained a reputation as more of a technocracy than a republic due to how many governing aspects it was given charge of. While space nomad groups like those Mia grew up among were perhaps the most outspoken denouncers of the AI, there was widely shared concern for the deep-rooted influence of the Philos Network, and how it could be leveraged. Her conversation with Electra had prompted Mia to wonder if her friends had been somehow brain-washed and, after she'd had a moment to calm down, asked, "Do you think it was Philosophia that might have had your memories wiped? I've heard of the AI doing that to people."

"It's certainly a possibility," said Electra calmly. "You should know, Aster and I are both missing things in the memory department, and we've had to come to peace with that. We could theorize all day about who and why. The only one who might be able to tell us is Xenos, and so far every time I've asked, he's only ever replied that he made a promise that he would tell me when the time was right, and that time hasn't come yet."

"Who is this Xenos?" asked Mia.

"He's our accountant," said Aster in a subdued voice, her gaze fixed distantly on the ship's controls.

"More to the point, he's the one you saw us speaking to," said Electra. "He can be kind of a pain, but if anyone can make sure this gets sorted out, it's him. You'll meet him when we get there."

"Does that mean you don't know your real names?" asked Mia.

"I suppose we've just used our callsigns for a while now, haven't we, Aster?" asked Electra, reflecting on the question.

"It can't be helped. Granted, such memories are insulating, but identic knowledge is less central to our beings than you think, Mia," said Aster. "We retain our skills, and I would argue our predispositions and tastes are more core to our personas than the labels we use for distinguishment."

"That's true," said Electra. "We use assumed names all the time, and it's not like we become completely different people even when we are acting. It's what you do that makes you the person you are, Mia, not the name."

Mia nodded in acknowledgment but found this comment strangely discomforting, perhaps because of the fact she knew her own name wasn't quite right, and she couldn't put her finger on why. After a moment she decided to dismiss it by changing the subject.

"So, just where are we heading?" she asked at length.

"The cradle of mankind . . . Terra," said Aster.

CHAPTER 3

To Hide on the Homeworld

"Terra," repeated Mia. "You mean *the* Earth?"

"The one and only," said Aster.

"I've never been to Earth," remarked Mia.

"Well then, this should be a pleasant experience," said Aster. "Granted, it is distant, but makes for one of the best hiding places for our purposes. Acceptable access to technological utilities, yet thanks to the last homeworld war, not so densely inhabited as to be without surveillance gaps or unlisted locations. It has plenty of abandoned districts and towns and is still peacefully contended by many colonial nations. Even the major powers only control a small fraction of Terra's landmass."

"Earth is . . . our original home?" asked Tyber.

"That's a good description," said Mia. "Our ancestors lived there."

"Why is it so sparsely inhabited then?"

"Well, it's kind of complicated," said Mia. Tyber's questions were simple, but they were rapidly serving as a reset in her perspective. Mia privately admired how

Tyber's straightforward approach had caused her to reexamine many things. For example, she had never thought about it, but megaships like *Megalodon* were a comparatively new advent, only a few generations old. Created from colony ships whose communities had chosen to wander between settled parts of space instead of settling new parts themselves, they were only viable now that mankind's settlement of space was no longer resembling a fairy circle expanding away from Earth.

"Earth used to put a lot more pressure on space colonies," said Mia after a pause, "to control them. Colonies didn't like that, so every time they extended their reach, they'd pack up and move further out into deep space."

Mia hadn't studied much history, but even she knew how the pattern had formed. When it had become clear how much people could accomplish apart from parasitic bureaucracy, most people couldn't escape it fast enough, and although the perils of outer space were numerous, the risks more than justified the reward."

"Aster mentioned war. What happened?" asked the tiger.

Mia shrugged. "I don't remember exactly how it happened, but Terran governments became unsustainable, and the planet's economy collapsed when some of the deep space colonies officially cut ties with them."

"Terra, for all its wealth, could not sustain the opulence and corruption of its governing bodies, and in a bid to retain power, war followed," Aster chimed in. "That war caused a collapse of Earth's infrastructure, and famine followed. What some call World War Three, or the last Homeworld War, scorched our planet. Understand, Tyber, to most deep space colonies, losing touch with the homeworld was like losing the light of a drowned candle at the center of a grand chandelier—minor, if not inconsequential."

"Yeah, I remember my grandparents often joking, 'If the colonies hadn't gone back for luxury goods, we might have forgotten the Earth altogether,'" Mia said with a chuckle.

"That's a rather accurate assessment, in all honesty," said Aster. "Earth still has a plethora of novelties that cannot be duplicated even with our advancements in technology. Plants and animal products of many kinds are desirable in space, and for all our rancor toward earthborne governments, the planet itself is still our collective home. In that regard, all spacefaring nations still prize Terra as the gem of mankind. However, politically speaking, the homeworld has become quite obsolete. It is tentatively governed by the colonies, who agree on very little except the desire to conserve Earth's natural beauty and balance. To preserve it as a model for habitability as we continue our own endeavors to terraform in space."

"That reminds me, doesn't Terra have a rather difficult customs system to get through? The last I heard, with every nation vying for a slice of our planet of origin, you need special permission from, well, just about everybody to set foot on it."

"I'm sure they can make an exception for us," said Aster with a gentle smile. "We have a special arrangement with Philosophia, which happens to be the designated controller of traffic to and from the surface."

"That's not a dangerous amount of power for an AI," Mia commented, the sarcasm in her tone unmistakable. "I can't make up my mind whether to be pleased or concerned."

"You could say we get a special pass to come and go as we please," inserted Electra smugly. "But yeah, it kind of scares me, too, sometimes."

"I concur, it's quite the confidence," commented Aster, "but given even those with a low opinion of Philosophia still trust it more than they trust each other, it is only to be expected. The important thing is its authority secures us discreet passage to a place few others can reach."

"Sounds like Earth belongs to Electra and Aster," said Tyber in a low voice.

"How so?" asked Mia.

"They're the only ones who get to come and go as they please," stated the tiger.

Aster said nothing, but Electra's response caused Mia to glance up as the agent nudged Aster and said, "Wipe that smirk off your face."

The ride there was uneventful, and Mia felt embarrassed she'd tried to threaten them. However, Electra and Aster seemed content to forget the incident, and more pleasant topics dominated their discussion the rest of the trip. Aster shared an exquisite array of snack foods, and Electra made an advance on her promise by searching the Philos Network with Mia for new clothes. Mia gathered what hints she could about her two friends but decided she owed it to them not to pry. They weren't agents of Philos per se, at least not directly. Electra had too many stories of working for private groups, or helping nations that hated the Philos Network, like the United Colonies of Caladria, and when Aster let slip that technically they were wanted by Philos's operations sector as fugitives, she felt Aster had given her a bigger hint about their association than she let on.

The site they went to was in the northern part of what had once been known as Colombia, but its cities were now almost completely overgrown ruins. As they came in for an approach, Mia glanced at their landing site to see what looked to be an estate nestled quietly in the valley. As they disembarked, Mia spotted the man they called Xenos waiting for them.

"Electra, it's been too long," he said, reaching to kiss her hand. Electra almost violently recoiled.

"I keep telling you to stop doing that!"

"My apologies," he said as he stretched his hand behind his head sheepishly. "You two must be Mia and Tyber. I hope your trip wasn't too taxing."

"Pleased to meet you, Mr. Xenos. You're . . . shorter than I expected," said Mia.

"I often have that effect in person," said the accountant with an awkward laugh. "Would you be more comfortable in the shade or the sun? I have cool drinks ready for everyone."

"The sun," said Mia and Tyber almost at once.

"Of course," said Xenos, "and please, just call me Samuel. Samuel Wilson. Xenos is more of a callsign for work."

The day was warm and bright, and Mia sipped her drink and enjoyed the open space. It was almost unnerving being out in such an open area, as it was such a departure from Megalodon's enclosed nooks, but it had its appeal too.

"So correct me if I'm mistaken on anything, but I summarize the situation thus," began Samuel. "You were taken to the black labs and kept there for an unlawfully extended test in the field of biografting, and Tyber here is a genetibeast who helped you to escape the lab. When Electra and Asterope found you, they resolved to help you escape your captors and took you with them on their ship."

"It's all accurate so far," said Mia.

Samuel scratched his head.

"I suppose it's a little late to point out that you two could have gone to *Megalodon*'s authorities to let them sort this out."

"Don't be ridiculous!" retorted Electra. "You know the moderators don't want to stick their necks out over the welfare of a sole citizen. They may tout that line about using 'sympathetic psychology' and 'cultural anthropology' to resolve problems without the so-called evils of 'police brutality,' but we both know they would rather have consigned her to slavery than expose that one of their commercial labs was up to no good."

"Besides, the last thing we needed was the attention of *Megalodon*'s law enforcement," commented Aster. "We pose a rather stiff security hazard, and even with the limited exposure we had, one of them came frighteningly close to identifying Electra."

"I concede you have a point there," said Samuel with a hint or resignation. "Unfortunately, this poses three problems we must resolve. First, Mia, you have seen Electra's and Asterope's capabilities and equipment. You probably realize by now they use quite a few things that aren't available to the general public. Second, your friend is a military grade genetibeast, and one who seems sapient at that. This complicates matters since artificially induced sapience is a difficult topic that is seldom handled well. Lastly, you both are wanted by certain parties within *Megalodon*, and this is perhaps the trickiest. Nomad collectives can hold spitefully long grudges, and that means you can't just wait it out until they stop looking for you."

Mia nodded at this and replied, "No. No I can't. I never expected to be part of a vendetta within my home ship, but now that I am, I'm developing a new appreciation for why people have such mixed opinions of space nomads. So what is it you recommend?"

"Well, I have a few avenues," he replied, pulling out a set of papers. "From what Electra tells me, you don't want to work for Philos."

"No sir," said Mia.

"Very well," said Samuel, setting the top paper aside. "Now, I could put you forward to some agencies I know within the Global Union or the Altaire Republic, but they each have their own foibles regarding genetically augmented creatures, so I suspect Tyber would not end up with you without a muzzle or handicap of some sort to reassure the public at large. I have contacts who could look into opportunities with other powers, but frankly these strike me as the best ones to ensure you're both treated right."

"It might sound callous, sir, but I'm indifferent what nation or power I'm part of," said Mia, "but I won't let anyone muzzle Tyber."

"I see. The second avenue I see involves giving you a new identity and relocating you. However, once again, this would not be as doable for Tyber, as he will tend to stand out. It would only be a matter of time before they recognized him and sought you both out. Tyber is of great value based on the intel I managed to squeeze off *Megalodon's* dark web. Since you intend to stay with Tyber, this is probably not the avenue you want to take either."

"N-No, I don't think so either," said Mia after a moment. "This will sound weird, but while I really want to shut the world out right now, spending time with Electra and Aster has shown me that I can't just *avoid* these problems."

"How do you come by that?" asked Electra with a tilt of her head.

Mia spoke haltingly, trying to find the words she needed.

"I don't quite know how to describe it, but while I was on the *Anawim*, I realized that with a ship like this and the skills you two have, you two really *could* hide from all kinds of trouble if you wanted, but you don't. You go out of your way to help others instead. I owe you both dearly for that. I want to be strong like that too. Stronger than my problems and free to help others, even if I have to take a risk from time to time."

"Well put, m'lady," said Tyber.

Mia thought she could see a grin forming on the edges of the accountant's mouth, as if he'd anticipated her response. Putting down his last page, he drew out another from his briefcase and said, "There is one more option. You could join a mercenary unit. I asked a friend of mine about the idea of taking on a genetibeast and its trainer within his ranks, and he sounded open to the idea. The advantage to this is while you won't be very hidden, you will be together and in time will earn the trust of some capable people who can look out for you. The nomad labs and their gangs would think twice before trying to target you on a ship loaded with dozens of heavily armed mercenaries. The disadvantage is the lifestyle. While they do some bighearted things, it's also wrought with risk. You'd be working as one of them, fighting alongside Tyber in some dicey situations. It may not be the safest occupation, but then again, maybe it would be."

"What happens if someone tries to legally claim Tyber as their own?" asked Mia. "Like through the Global Union's interstellar courts or something?"

"I strongly doubt *Megalodon* will attempt legal action. That would require showing proof he was created by them, and that would implicate them in their crimes against you two. The most likely action they would take in that event is to accuse you of creating or mistreating Tyber, and we can avoid that by manufacturing an appropriate story to justify your partnership. Since the black labs did the hard part of erasing your identity, supplying you with a new one will be comparatively easy. If any of them were to reveal your past, you might even get some vindication out of it all, since it would open the door to tell how you escaped," Samuel said, then paused for effect before adding, "*by yourselves*, if you follow my meaning."

"You mean you want us to leave Electra and Aster's role out of any story we might tell," said Mia.

"Yes. To briefly put it. It would be a great favor to me, and I will happily extend my services to you in exchange for your discreet omissions. You would merely contact Philos corporate by any means you like, give your name, and tell them you have a message for me and use my callsign, Xenos. One of us will find *you* then."

"It sounds perfect, except . . ." Mia balled her hands into fists on her knees.

"Except we both know Tyber is sentient . . .er sapient," she said, stumbling slightly over her words. "He deserves to be treated with the same dignity as you or I. Not as a beast with a trainer."

"That's true," said Samuel with a nod. He clasped the edge of his jaw. "But easier said than done. I cannot simply declare him sapient without a vast network of people shining a spotlight on him. It's a controversial topic, artificially induced sapience. It is one many people are eager to see handled responsibly but are divided on what ought to happen. Perhaps the gentlest way to convince others without putting him under excessive scrutiny is to demonstrate it in your interaction with him. Treat him right, and in time your peers will follow, and then society. What do you think, Tyber? Do you find letting Mia carry the title of 'handler' for you palatable for the time being?"

"Quite," said Tyber.

"How can *you* go along with this?" asked Mia irately.

"M'lady, the man isn't trying to be hurtful. He's trying to be realistic," said Tyber. "It is a title. Nothing more. It changes nothing between us."

"I'm afraid it's not the first time I've had to compromise with a half truth for a viable solution," said Samuel. "I wish I could offer you better. However, the decision is still yours. I cannot make you choose one of these, nor tell you how best to live your life from this point forward."

Mia nodded after a long pause, then asked Samuel, "Can we walk for a moment?"

The accountant acquiesced, and the two went for a short stroll. When they were out of earshot, Mia asked, "How do you know Electra and Aster?"

"We go quite far back. Further than you would expect," said Samuel.

"Are you some kind of Philos handler for them? I'm not stupid. It's clear you're more than just their accountant."

"Handler implies a lot of control I would never presume to exert," said Samuel with a slightly nervous smile. "I'm more like their . . . liaison."

"Why did Philosophia seal away their memories?"

"I'm rather surprised they spoke to you about their memories at all. You're worried you won't see them again if you join the mercenaries, aren't you?" replied Samuel.

"Right now, they're the only friends I feel I can rely on," said Mia.

"I could ask for them to shadow you for a time, pose as mercenaries themselves while you transition. I have instructions for them to lie low for a few weeks as it is."

"That would be nice, but you're trying to change the topic," said Mia. "You still didn't answer my question. I surfed the Philos Network earlier today and learned that officially speaking, they're wanted by Philos and the Global Union, but it's already clear they're working with Philos to some degree. Electra told me they lost their memories at some point. If the AI didn't erase their minds, then who did and why?"

"Shrewd questions, all of them," he said with a glance back at Electra, who sat a distance off. "You remind me of her, you know, and that's as high a compliment as I give anyone. However, I'm afraid you'll have to learn the answer to those questions on your own. Don't let it discourage you from trying, though. That's the thing about secrets; just because they can't be shared doesn't mean they aren't to be found. Now, correct me if I'm wrong, but I think you've already made up your mind on what you want to do next, haven't you?"

"I have," said Mia.

"Good. Then let's head back. Electra and Asterope are good sports, but they can only feign disinterest for so long."

CHAPTER 4

To Become Strong

What followed bored even Tyber at times, but Samuel did his best to make the paperwork engaging and easy on Mia, and she appreciated the sheer amount of effort that must have been mustered to quickly prepare things for the transition she was about to undertake. The mercenary group Samuel suggested was small, but of good repute, and well equipped for what it was. They called themselves the Rail Drivers, and they had been formed by veteran soldiers who wanted to pull in a larger paycheck to support the underprivileged they constantly found in the aftermath of conflict. A notion that had gained it the support of many major groups, including Samuel's associates within Philos Corporate and many of its partners. It was clear that Philos and the AI would continue to be names she was going to hear regularly; however, that was a far cry from having to work for them, and all in all, Mia was grateful the accountant had sought to be so straightforward with her on the matter.

"Captain Rikeman happens to be an acquaintance of mine," stated Samuel. "He served with the Caladrian military and knows the battlefield as well as anyone in the industry. Now, I'll only make this offer because you are a friend, but I can arrange for a line of credit to let you obtain a cerebral interface—"

"No thank you," said Mia before the accountant could finish. "I may even regret that I didn't take you up on that offer someday. I've heard you really are on a social handicap without one, but setting the social impact aside, I remember multiple times when I was grateful I wasn't rigged with a programmable implant, even a basic one."

Mia then gestured to her ears, pulling on them slightly.

"If those monsters on *Megalodon* could do this to my body, I shudder to imagine what they might have done to my brain if I'd given them a way to link it with a computer."

"I'd rather not think about it either. I cringe every time these two go into action because I know it all too well," said Samuel, pointing to Electra and Aster. "I don't think it will pose a problem, though. The captain of the Rail Drivers isn't particularly opposed to cybernetics, but he doesn't gravitate to them himself either. You'll be pleased to learn he probably has similar notions to you on the matter."

"I think your choice shows great prudence, Mia," said Aster.

This remark caught Mia by surprise, as "Asterope, the tech wizard," was the last one she expected this comment from. Electra and Samuel's agreement confounded her, and as the evening set in, Mia's tired mind swam to make sense of it. Perhaps Samuel had spotted this, for he suggested they turn in early, then had the girls lead Mia to a furnished room so large Tyber could turn in it. It was getting to be fun, getting all the space in the world to relax in, but this was only a mild comfort as she pondered her friends' comments along with the rest of what had transpired that day.

From there, the next weeks demanded Mia's fullest effort. Training to fit her new role as a mercenary animal trainer was a harrowing task, but Mia was confident she could make it work. It helped that Electra had volunteered to train her in self-defense and weapon handling. As they rotated between stretching, running, sparring, and exercising, Mia discovered a newfound dexterity she'd never experienced before, possibly as an unexpected benefit of her alterations. Regardless, it felt liberating to be healthy and strong again, and Electra was an excellent teacher.

Training Tyber to work with her was another challenge. Whatever method had allowed Tyber to speak had given him some basic grasp of ranks, commands, and tactics. Yet for all these useful concepts, Tyber had never actually hunted for himself and found the process a diverting puzzle and a challenge. Often, Mia had to watch with Electra from afar through a set of goggles or binoculars that showed him in otherwise invisible spectrums of light. It was a handy tool, and except for the fact Tyber was learning the sneaking and stalking part faster than she was, it was a joy to watch him develop his natural predatory skills.

"Notice how he plans his approach," said Electra as they watched at one point. "Half of survival is spotting a potential threat and staying ahead of it. It's also often the difference between being predator and prey. As the handler and person in charge, you will need to think an extra step ahead of Tyber, for his sake as well as your own."

Mia couldn't help but reflect on the idea. She'd never really had to think this way before, except perhaps in the social sense of things. *Megalodon* had a hypersocial component in how it approached keeping order so that how you made yourself out to look or act could often curb a problem before it began, making navigating through the more rigid aspects of its social hierarchies easier. Mia had always considered herself fairly socially adept in that regard, for before her time in the black labs, she'd known how to make others comfortable around her, and it had won her most of the things she'd wanted. Yet regrettably, it had served her poorly when she'd been at her most vulnerable. She knew she would have to develop new ways to tackle such problems, and she couldn't deny her intense desire to stay by Tyber's side now. Tyber had been the only one to stick with her through that dark time, although he'd had little more choice in the matter than she did.

Three attempts and as many hours later, Tyber loped up with his trophy of success and was quite disappointed when they declined to partake of his bounty. However, he got over this quickly. Aster would occasionally ask Tyber to show off his other capabilities, which were impressive, to say the least.

"He has at least twice the physical capabilities of any normal tiger," she noted at one point to Mia. "My guess is they used *puma concolor* DNA as their primary genetic splice for him."

"Wouldn't that be a step down?" asked Mia between pull-ups. "I thought pumas were smaller than tigers."

"In this case, *puma concolor* refers to cougars. And yes, they are smaller," said Aster. "However, the cougar is of the 'small cat' lineage. Pound for pound, small cats have nearly twice the physical prowess of their 'large cat' cousins of genus *panthera*, which includes lions and tigers. If given the same mass and reach as a tiger, a cougar would be overwhelmingly strong. I expect this is what they aimed to supply Tyber with when they made him. Simple and frighteningly effective. It would appear they reinforced his skeletal frame to support this power as well."

"When did you learn all this?" asked Electra.

"I did some homework while you two sculpted," said Aster with a subtle smile. "With the Philos Network at my fingertips, I can learn in six hours as much as anyone with a degree in the same field. Mia will need some of these details if she wants to look after Tyber, and we have to fill in as many blanks as we can for her, given we wrecked the laboratory in question."

"Your parents must have been crazy intellectual or something," commented Electra. "My head would hurt studying six hours of *anything* in a day!"

Training progressed steadily, and Electra's teaching was kind but ruthless, for she never gave Mia an inch when pushing her to try things again. Perhaps the concept was new, but Mia realized one night that she would have given up if it had been anyone but Electra pushing her so hard. Learning to pace herself during close combat training was counterintuitive, and Electra had to remind her more than once that her own bionic body didn't tire like hers and that it was important to gauge her stamina. Later, when the dull pains from earlier in the day raged, it became a challenge in the reverse as Electra pushed her not to stop or slow down despite her mounting exhaustion.

"This isn't just training for a fight, Mia. It's training for how to get along in a big, bad world that doesn't take excuses," said Electra at one point. "This is the bare minimum you're going to need if you want to face problems like this, and the Rail Drivers can only do so much to help you if you can't do every. . . single. . . thing I'm teaching you and Tyber to do."

"Was this how you trained?" asked Mia, trying to conceal a desperate plea for mercy in the question.

"No, I trained first under a lax wimp who set me up to fail. Then I trained under a maniac who specialized more in mind games than teaching a sound method. I went through five instructors before I met someone capable, and he was the one who taught me that only those who can do it for themselves are fit to teach. Trust me, Mia, the only reason I'm pushing you is because I know first-hand how necessary it is if you really want this!"

Target practice proved the hardest part of each day, although this was to be expected. Electra deliberately reserved these sessions for the end of each day, when every muscle ached and wobbled and the firearms felt their heaviest and hardest to steady.

"If you can learn to aim when you're like this, you'll be able to shoot it anywhere," she would comment. "Now, from the standing position again."

Mia practiced, learning each new weapon and tool Electra showed her. She looked back on her outburst on the ship and felt increasingly thankful she hadn't fired Electra's forty-five handgun. The times she fired weapons like it, she'd found the high caliber hard to control even with proper instruction. However, Electra's choice of sidearm had also become a personal goal for Mia. More than just her mentor's favored weapon, Electra considered it the ideal balance of power and control to use when she wanted to *save* a life. Since skill memory was where the majority of Electra's memories predating her days as a posthuman came from, it had an intriguing and appealing effect on Mia.

Then, about halfway through their training, Electra's tasks and assignments shifted. Tyber and Mia would be tasked to "catch" one another, often with the goal of tagging the other with a flag or chalk pad, and Mia was not fond of it. Even when Tyber wasn't stalking her back, he had a slight edge, but more often than not, they caught on to one another's presence before they could even get close, at which Tyber would rush her, although sometimes Mia would manage to get Tyber with her tag by throwing it. Yet with each try, new tactics started dawning to Mia: She could read wind, and Tyber's overreliance on scent dominated his mindset, making it easier to lure him places. However, truth be told, she could only gauge her success by how startled Tyber would be when he did pick up that she was getting close, for he had an uncanny way of detecting someone's presence that bordered on a sixth sense.

It was not until Mia had reached the point of sometimes "catching" Tyber like this that Electra started getting even harder on them, citing at length the places they'd given themselves away, growing critical of even Tyber for his laxness, making Mia wonder who was really getting trained. Then one day Mia brought it up in complaint.

"Look, I'm almost to where I can catch Tyber, Electra. How much better do you want me to be?"

"It's a nice start, but you've still got a ways to go," said Electra. "We're in a benign environment compared to some of the ones he may have to work in. Tyber isn't used to this, and as glad as I am that you're reaching his level, you both have a ways to go before you can do this right."

"You think *Tyber* isn't good enough?" asked Mia. "I'll remind you, he took down more than one guard back on *Megalodon* before we even met you, and he's picked up how to stalk prey like a natural!"

"I know you think we're into advanced training because you can sneak up on Tyber from time to time, Mia, but this is still the basics," maintained Electra.

"Basics? Really? How much longer are you going to drill with me on this? You think we can't take care of ourselves like we are now?" asked Mia in challenge.

"If you're ready for the real world, you'll need to do more than entertain me," said Electra, a slight tone of indignance creeping into her voice.

In that instant, Electra vanished. Mia wasn't sure if she'd moved or engaged some kind of high-tech cloaking technology, but the result had been apparent, for it had caught Mia off guard. Sounds like small gunshots rang from nearby trees, causing Mia's head and eyes to dart about to assess what was happening, and she'd barely caught on to the fact they were stones hitting the trees when she felt Electra make four different pokes or pinches to her torso, followed by the sensation of her tail getting pulled out of her pants. It was unsettling and humiliating, and Mia turned to stop it only to feel her left foot slip out from under her as she shifted her weight, turning her over and causing her to tumble. Tyber roared as he swiped the air impotently, backing up only to catch on something thin that restrained his back leg, aggravating him terribly. As he shook his foot to get it free, Mia scrambled up and moved to see what he'd been caught on.

"Your left side is open," Mia heard Electra whisper in her ear. Mia turned to face her left, only to feel herself being pushed headlong from what had been her right side in a simple misdirection, then stopped again as Electra gripped the end of her tail and pulled her back to her feet before slapping her on the behind. Mia yelled in objection and swung in aggravation, but suddenly found herself getting pulled by the ears under Tyber and, too surprised to make a concerted effort to fight it, sliding headfirst under him. A second later, she felt Tyber's weight on her as his front paw slipped out from under him, causing him to drop to the ground.

Electra may or may not have truly "vanished" initially, but she *had* been visible for the brief moments while they'd skirmished, and it had clearly been to illustrate she'd not actually had to hide to get the job done. Most humiliatingly, Electra hadn't moved very fast or used a great deal of force to overpower them. As she brushed Mia's hair back, Electra stared down at her with a cold, almost pained expression on her face as she spoke.

"People who get to you will use your senses, your feelings, and almost certainly your alterations to manipulate you! They'll make you feel naked while fully clothed and abused before they've laid a finger on you! They'll get in your head and turn you inside out with every dirty trick in the book, and then . . . then they'll get nasty! That's what Xenos meant when he said the lifestyle you're taking on will be a challenge, Mia. This is a high-risk profession, and there's no safety net for failure. You and Tyber are going to fight people who train their whole lives to be the absolute worst!"

Mia fought back her anger and frustration but found herself giving way to tears. She hadn't felt so toyed with since the black labs, and it hurt to even think about it. Electra wasted no time in unwrapping Tyber from what looked to be a section of cord that had come from Mia's survival kit before helping the two of them up. Mia knew each touch and act could have been a terrible, if not lethal, blow as it all settled in. Mia heard Electra help Tyber up and, as she stood up herself, felt the posthuman gently stroking her ears, as if in apology for pulling on them earlier.

"I'm sorry if I went too far, Mia," said Electra, "but I can't stress how important it is not to get cocky at this stage! You and Tyber are actually very good at this, but there are tricks and methods I haven't introduced to you yet, and now that you're aware of it, you probably realize you're going to need to be ready for every one of them if you don't want to get caught off guard."

Tyber seemed at a loss for words as he muttered, "That was . . ."

"That was a lot to take in," said Mia with a shiver, feeling more astonished than anything. In a sense, she realized she'd known of all the moves Electra had pulled. Dirty fighting was a staple on *Megalodon*, and while she'd generally only spectated such things, Mia knew Electra's long series of "sucker punch" moves had been executed more as an act of exposition and not as a serious attempt to hurt her. Still, she couldn't help but clutch each place she'd been struck, like she'd nearly been impaled by each jab.

"I know," said Electra apologetically. "I'd planned to introduce you to some of these one at a time, but I guess I went a little overboard. I hope you'll forgive me for messing with your ears and tail, but you have to be ready for your enemies to do that. Truce?"

Mia nodded acquiescently but refused to look up for a time.

CHAPTER 5

The New Starts

Training progressed steadily. When Samuel arrived with the shuttle, he seemed preoccupied but was still pleased to bring them their ordered goods. It was the last "run" of several that he'd made, and among this lot, there were some basics Mia would need for her new life, including select clothes and requested luxuries: some basic cosmetics, a proper carrying bag, select treats (for both her and Tyber), and a hair dryer (which had actually been Tyber's request). Along with these, Samuel provided her a new wrist display and the trappings of an identity that went with it.

As Samuel arrayed the birth certificate, Altairan citizenship ID card, and other assorted pages and identifying numbers she would be memorizing, she found herself in mental disassociation with it, for despite the effort she knew had gone into them, they all seemed incredulous and artificial.

"I wish I could say a reformed identity gets easier with time, but at least most of this is based on what you remember of your original identity," said Samuel sympathetically.

The last gifts were those chosen by Electra and Aster, and they would be for her new work as a mercenary. They included some select weapons, a new protective layer of body armor, and a matching harness customized for Tyber.

"I wanted this to arrive earlier, but I think you'll like this," said Electra as she held up a hooded mantle against the armored outfit. "This hood has properties akin to my cybernetic body's exterior. Not only will it provide some excellent protection, but it will hide your signature from all manner of detection systems. I wanted to get you the same optical camouflage we use, but Xenos insisted I get you something that was available on the open market."

"The best optic camouflage in the world won't do her any good if it develops a fault and nobody knows how to fix it," said Samuel as he tried to shrug off Electra's sidelong glare.

"Whatever. It will still make you virtually invisible," she said with a wink. "I'll show you how to maintain it tomorrow, and—"

"I'm afraid she will have to settle for a written guide and the manual. It seems the furlough for the Rail Driver Mercenary Company is being cut short," said Samuel.

"So suddenly? You told me we had at least three more days!" Electra objected.

"Rikeman's company has been given an advanced retainer to show up at the surface complex on Kiito in a week, and she will need to join them before they take off tomorrow morning."

Electra responded by driving her heel into the ground in frustration.

"I don't favor the situation either," said Samuel with a shrug,

"I sense 'Sophia's behind this," said Electra.

"That's certainly plausible, particularly since the AI also requested you two to intercept some data related to Mia and Tyber at the same time," the accountant replied, pointing to Electra and Aster.

"A mission that could secure Mia's and Tyber's medical logs. The only mission that could pull us away. I see what you mean," said Aster.

"Well, it's gratifying to see the AI is as shrewd as ever," said Electra sarcastically.

"I mention this because this might be the last chance you get to see each other again," said Samuel.

"That's not fair. We both know 'Sophia has no say in who we choose to associate with between missions," said Electra hotly.

Samuel did not respond to this, but merely glanced back at the ship and replied, "I'll be on board when you are ready to go, Mia."

"Well, then I suppose I don't get the chance to present this to you the way I planned to, but I want you to have this," said Electra as she removed her belt and, gripping the handgun in its holster, handed it to Mia.

"Your forty-five . . . but I'm still terrible with it," Mia stammered.

"You're going to do fine. It seemed appropriate to give you this, given its history with us. You're a better shot than you give yourself credit for Mia. A little more practice and exercise, and I really think you'll be a force to reckon with," said Electra. "Just stick to the routine we discussed. I'm positive your new teammates will be able to help you too."

The girls hugged each other good-bye, and donning the belt, Mia reluctantly boarded the shuttle. She found Samuel staring wistfully ahead as she stepped into the cabin, and the assistant at the controls initiated the takeoff procedure. Tyber nestled himself between the seats, hoping a low profile would keep him from feeling airsick.

"I guess this means they won't be joining me there," said Mia as she watched her friends through the window.

"If it turns out the information relates to Tyber as we expect it does, it may end up being exceedingly helpful to you, with the added benefit of denying its makers their records. That's why those two are looking into the matter," assured Samuel. "I wish that could make up for things."

"Does the AI pull this trick often," asked Mia, "manipulating the situation to get its way on something?"

"You make it sound like a conspiracy theory. Philosophia, whatever else you think of it, is not self-aware . . . at least not in the sense you or I am. Many people don't like to admit this, but self-awareness is based on purpose, and the AI's core directive or 'purpose' is not like our own."

"Aren't you worried it will turn on its makers?"

"That's certainly the popular concern. However, my misgivings lie more with the dependency we, the end users, place on it without understanding it. Philosophia is given countless objectives and parameters, many of which are mutually exclusive, if not outright contradictory. It will never miss a trick to fulfill each and every objective it can, but therein lie many of its risks . . . and limitations. I personally glean a great deal of entertainment from its directive to maintain and improve its public standing. It really gives me no end of humor to watch as it plays out."

"How so?" asked Mia.

Samuel smiled and, taking a second to gather his thoughts, said, "Let me put it another way: Imagine if you had the foresight to mitigate two catastrophes, but you knew that if you didn't prevent the first, lesser one, people would learn from it and posture their state of mind more appropriately for the next one. They would become more independent, which would actually enable you to mitigate the greater disaster even better. You even know that the net number of lives saved would be greater than if you'd prevented the first. But then it would also damage people's trust if they found out you'd done this. Would you risk your track record and save some extra lives in the long run, or opt to retain the trust of the people and let them take their extra lumps unknowingly, aware that retaining their trust would prove valuable, even if achieved by false pretense?"

"I-I may need to hear the question again," said Mia. "No, I take it back. I'm not sure I could answer it even then."

"I understand. I'm acclimated to it, and the question remains difficult even for me," said Samuel. "However, it gives you a vague idea of the ways the AI has to work to fulfill its primary directive."

"And what is its primary directive?" asked Mia.

"Why, to protect and serve mankind," Samuel replied. "Theoretically, that's been its directive from its inception. However, even if we were to assume that *was* the primary end the AI worked toward, it could still come off as unreliable, insidious, or suspect, and while it has to weigh those perceptions in its behavior, perception isn't its highest priority. Take your relationship with Electra and Aster. To it, that bond you three share and its impact on others is merely one such cluster of factors. If you think about your situation, what you perceive as a ploy to drive you apart could just as likely be trying to draw you closer together. Regardless, it cannot make you do anything you don't want to, so ultimately you have to be the one to decide your future for yourself. In my experience, the only time Philosophia goes against a person's will is when it is practical, which is far more seldom than you might think."

"I still don't trust it," said Mia bitterly.

"I respect that, much like I can respect your choice to forgo the cerebral implant, even if I did offer it," said Samuel, glancing sidelong and flashing a broad grin.

"You know, I never got around to thanking you properly," said Mia, softened by his infectious, albeit somewhat unsettling, smile. "You know me the least, and yet I doubt I'll ever actually grasp how much effort you've put into helping me."

"Few things are more gratifying to me than helping those who work hard to better their situation," said Samuel, closing his eyes and facing forward. "Make these efforts work for you, and who knows, I may yet owe you a favor or two someday."

Mia smiled back at this remark and tried to relax and enjoy the rest of the flight. Occasionally, she would ask him a question about the people she would be working with, but for the most part she felt content to let her mind wander as they flew.

They arrived late that night, circling the freighter the mercenaries were loading up on before landing. Now that she was here, Mia found herself strangely giddy to meet her new peers. Small craft sped overhead as she walked across with Tyber, holding a few of her bags. Crew stopped and waved as they spotted her. Apparently, she was expected.

A young man stopped his work on a small generator and approached her.

"A beautiful creature, ma'am. I take it you're the new trainer we were expecting?"

"That's me. The name is . . ." Mia closed her eyes, concentrating so she would avoid mewling as she said, "Mia." The attempt was only partially successful.

"My name is Eli, short for Elias," the young man replied, then pointed at Mia's ears then at Tyber, smiling. "I sense a theme going on. I take it you like cats?"

"Something like that," said Mia, brushing her hair back self-consciously as a second, younger crew member ran up to shake her hand.

"You must be the genetibeast trainer," she said with a bright smile. "I'm Lynlee. We heard you'd be coming with a genetibeast, but a white tiger? Wow!"

"I take it he's fine to wander free with you?" asked Eli as others closed in.

Mia glanced at Samuel, who gave a knowing wink. Apparently, he'd kept the details to a minimum for her amusement.

Smirking, she leaned against Tyber and this time didn't even try to pronounce her name right as she announced, "Yes, I'm Mia. Let me introduce you to my partner, Tyber."

"Is he safe? He looks so tame," said Lynlee. "His fur looks so soft!"

"Would you like to say hello?" Mia asked, trying to build for a surprise.

However Lynlee blushed and asked, "Is it okay if I pet him behind the ear?"

"Well, I think that's up to Tyber, isn't it?" said Mia as she glanced down, stroking Tyber as she did. The tiger nodded and stepped forward. Lynlee held out her hand gently, and Tyber sniffed before stroking his head against it endearingly. The teen made a squeal of delight as she pet him gently.

"You smell . . . floral," he said suddenly.

Lynlee jumped back in surprise. A wave of shock and mirth rippled out at this new development, and those only half watching before suddenly dropped everything to see their entertaining new members.

"You big meanie! You didn't tell me he could *talk*!" said Lynlee with a cry of joy as she gently pushed Mia, who couldn't stop giggling. "Oh my gosh! You're so fluffy and sweet I could die!"

A gruff voice bellowed over the intercom of the ship, "All right, all right. You've all seen our newest members. They're crewmates, not mascots, so stop gawking like we've joined the damn circus! We've got a tight schedule to keep. Once we're underway, I'm sure there will be plenty of time to say hello and pet the nice kitty."

The crowd reluctantly dispersed as the broad-shouldered man who had made the announcement pocketed his microphone. He sported a golden horseshoe mustache along with a receding hairline cut to a short length. He had a hefty build that would have been imposing even without the battery of muscles beneath his shirt, and his skin had the tan and glow of manual labor. The wear on his clothes matched, giving him the appearance of a hardworking man. As he approached, he crossed his arms and said, "So, Steve, are these the two you told me about?"

"The name is Samuel," corrected the accountant.

"Right, right. And these two?"

"Yes, this is them," said Samuel with a resigned smile. "Mia, Tyber, let me introduce Captain Jack Rikeman, friend and distinguished leader of the Rail Driver Mercenary Company. They glean the name both from the hypermagnetic rail mass driver, which they frequent on their heavy infantry, vehicles, and mech units, and as a nod to their freight partners who furnish them transport and a mobile refuge."

"That's right. Say hello to our home on the go: the star freighter *John Henry*. I'm sorry to pull you here early, but when one of our crews gets a request, we can't generally afford to sit on it. I don't have time to give you the kid treatment, and if I know this number cruncher, he's probably talked your ear off already, so I'll make this brief: We're a busy crew that works as a team. I've been briefed on your basic training, and I know you're new to the field. I actually prefer it that way, since it means you haven't had as much chance to work any bad habits into your routine yet. Ours will be a give-and-take relationship: What you want from this job will hinge on what you bring to it. If you need results, you better deliver them. If you want answers, you better be asking questions. Is that arrangement good for ya?"

"Yes, sir," said Mia almost instinctively.

"And you?" asked the captain. His gaze fell on Tyber, catching the tiger in a yawn.

Tyber sat up, pleased to find he, too, had been addressed, and replied, "No objections."

"Good. You two have already met Lynlee. Go track her down and have her help you get settled aboard. We're not a boys' club, but this isn't generally work that draws in the ladies, so be sure to take note where the girl's section begins and ends. I won't be held responsible for any catcalls if you wander into the common area in your towel a week from now."

"Catcalls? Really?" said Mia, annoyed.

"What? No, I . . . Just go find Lynlee and have her help you unload," said Jack with a grunt.

Not inclined to stay annoyed, Mia left Jack with Samuel, or "Steve," as Jack kept calling him, and went looking for Lynlee, who was only too happy to escort them to their quarters.

"Come on aboard, and welcome to the *John Henry*! Oh, I'm so excited!" gushed Lynlee. As Lynlee chattered away, Mia found herself evaluating the girl. She was young—younger than anyone Mia had expected to meet on the trip. She was dressed in cargo shorts and a tool belt, and by age, she looked to be no older than fourteen, prompting her to wonder what had drawn her aboard a ship like this.

"This is the first time Jack has taken a genetibeast on as part of the crew. He always says, 'That's the last industry we need to be contributing to,' but from what I heard, he made an exception for you. Maybe it's because Tyber is so well behaved."

Tyber made no remark at this but exchanged a quizzical glance with Mia.

"This is our bunkroom," said Lynlee as they entered the room. "There aren't a lot of us, so pick whichever empty bunk you like best. Mine is the top bunk there with the stuffed sloth."

"Oh, then I'll take the one under you," said Mia, tossing her bag on the empty bunk beneath.

"Oh," said Lynlee nervously, "I'd love that, but I should give fair warning that I'm a rough sleeper," then added sheepishly, "I tend to drape over the edge at night, and there have been complaints."

"I grew up on *Megalodon*. I've lived most of my life with roommates sleeping so close you could tell when they last bathed or brushed their teeth," said Mia with a relaxed stretch. "Honestly, sleeping alone reminds me a little too much of the black labs, so a noisy sleepyhead hanging over the edge will be a comfort."

Lynlee grinned at Mia's remark and, unable to find words, jumped up and down with excitement and wrapped herself around Mia in a heartfelt hug. Mia smiled and returned the hug awkwardly. They were going to get along just fine.

"So what happened at the black labs?" asked a voice from behind.

Mia had heard the footsteps striding in behind her from the hall as they'd been speaking, and turned to see a woman in the entryway. She wore glasses and a lab coat, indicative of a medic of some sort. Mia knew it wasn't fair to judge the doctor before she'd even met her, but she could tell she was getting agitated, so she chose to dodge the inquiry by simply saying, "Oh. Hello."

"Oh, hi doc! Mia, this is our other regular roommate, Dr. Valerie Garnier. She's assistant head physician aboard the *John Henry*. She looks after most of us and coordinates our paramedics from the ship," said Lynlee.

The doctor seemed to intuit Mia's feelings, for she took a small step back before offering a courteous handshake and saying in an apologetic tone, "I'm afraid I'm the physician on duty right now, so I can only stay for a moment. Still, it's a pleasure to meet you. I wanted a chance to say hello and welcome you aboard. If there's anything I can do to help, just let me know."

"Thanks. I will," Mia said, then waved good-bye.

Lynlee was cheery, and the two girls idly swapped stories on daily life and experiences as they rallied to retrieve Mia's gear.

The luggage took little time to load, and Lynlee ran ahead with the last of it when Samuel pulled Mia aside to be sure she had the information she needed to contact him.

"I hope you don't find this presumptuous, but Asterope and I did some tweaking to your wrist display's firmware," said Samuel, "and added some useful reading material if you feel so inclined."

"Aster thinks of everything, doesn't she?" As Samuel turned away to leave, Mia added, "Oh, Mr. Wilson, sir?"

"Yes?"

"When do you intend to tell Electra and Aster about their pasts?" she asked.

"I'm afraid that would be . . . a secret," said Samuel with an impish smile.

"You don't ever intend to restore their memories, do you?" said Mia flatly.

"You're wrong. I look forward to that day more than anything else," said Samuel soberly, bowing slightly and gently waving good-bye. Then he turned and disappeared into the shuttle. He took his seat beside the adjutant pilot and stared as Mia sauntered back toward the mercenary ship.

"Did something happen down there?" asked the android pilot.

"Nothing of consequence, Rho. I think people can be very cruel without knowing it sometimes, don't you?" commented Samuel.

CHAPTER 6

The *John Henry*

Mia hoped her halcyon days with Electra and Aster weren't over, but for the moment, she knew she had to look ahead to what was to come. After stashing the last of her goods for takeoff, she buckled in alongside Lynlee and felt the craft gently lurch with its initial takeoff. The ship was underway. When the all-clear was extended for the crew to move about again, Jack called Mia into a conference room to brief her.

"Our job is a brief one, but it ought to give you a good chance to learn the basics without getting thrown into the thick of it. We're supplementing station security at a facility on Kiito. It's a planetoid in an asteroid belt, and they station themselves near its surface for the mild gravity well, as it assists in processing ore," explained Rikeman. "It's had a few growth spurts in the last decade, and we're often the ones the station's council hires as a prevention measure to ensure there's no spike in crime or violence or union shenanigans as they transition to push for perks and bonuses."

"You think they'll get violent?" asked Mia.

"Not if they have any sense," said Rikeman with a selective grunt. "My friend Tim is a former Rail Driver who retired to this place half a year ago, and based on his description, the leadership of this facility has been doing the job well. Still, don't underestimate the power of stupidity, especially when people are congregated in a tight space. I mentioned you and your partner to the command staff, and they were eager to see you work with their security guards. The families there would enjoy a change of pace, and you'll certainly be that. I gather from what Wilson said that Tyber can handle himself and won't get out of control, but please brief him on the trouble he might encounter."

"I'm confident Tyber won't pose a problem," assured Mia.

"Can he subdue a fleeing suspect without injuring them?" inquired Rikeman.

"We've never tried that before specifically, but I'm confident he's capable. I'll work with him to make sure he retains a soft touch if that's what you're worried about."

"Very good. Then that just leaves getting your gear fitted for the part and eventually getting you set up for a space suit. That's the other reason I insisted you join us for this mission. Remember that retired friend I mentioned earlier? He manufactures our unit's space suits. He's one of the few who knows how to make them to our specifications, and I want you to have one if you're going to work with us for very long."

"Space suit?" asked Mia. "I know it might be shocking, but even though I've lived in space most of my life, I don't actually have a lot of experience working in outer space environments or zero gravity."

"Consider this a chance to learn. It's a standard component for every Rail Driver," said Rikeman. "Part of our agreement with the *John Henry* is protection against boarding. It's only a matter of time before you'll need one, and you certainly don't want to go without if you do a lot of ship travel. Think of this as an on-the-job training session. I'll be watching to evaluate your skills and how to fit you into our crew. I've never had a geneti-beast trainer on board, and frankly, until Wilson talked me into taking you on, I'd been against it. The fact your tiger friend is intelligent and you aren't exactly *training* him is the main reason I made an exception. Still, you're responsible for him. To the extent that I can, I'll see he's treated as a crew member, but if Tyber causes trouble, the consequences will ultimately fall on you. Also: You're pulling your own weight independently. I grant, there are concessions for the unique nature of your role, but as Wilson probably explained to you, I can't afford an armchair mercenary. You're not from a military background, so expect to be barked at. When you're ordered to do something, I expect you to jump on it like it's about to scurry away. Now, I have your shipboard duties listed here as well as the times and crew members you'll be meeting with to prep. Don't miss any of them."

"I'll do my best, sir!" said Mia confidently, only to feel her ears twitch nervously as if they were intent on making a show of her apprehension.

"Then we'll just have to see what your best looks like," said Rikeman. "Don't forget to check the *John Henry*'s duty roster every day as well. We're not passengers on this ship; we're crew, and we need to be compliant with whatever Captain Stratweiss demands while we're aboard her ship."

When Jack was finished, Mia made her exit and met Tyber in the hall.

"And where were you? I was worried I was going to get a call that you were loose and preventing us from launching. Did you hide somewhere?"

"I thought about it, but Eli was kind enough to provide me a suitable place for takeoff."

"That's good to hear. Wait, who's Eli?" asked Mia.

"This one. Don't you remember him?" said Tyber, turning to the man striding up next to him. Mia looked up and recognized him as the man who'd first introduced himself when she'd disembarked the shuttle with Samuel.

"Oh. Well, thanks," said Mia sheepishly to the technician. "I'll be honest, I hadn't thought through this takeoff with Tyber very well, and, well, while my partner is generally pretty good about space travel, he isn't keen on small spaces, so any effort to keep him out of a kennel means a lot to both of us."

"Not a problem," replied Eli. "I'll be honest too—I was gratified Tyber chose to ask me about it. Most new crewmen just try to improvise something themselves, and I'm left cleaning up the mess."

Mia faltered, feeling somewhat embarrassed at the imposition, and she'd completely forgotten his name.

"Still, I appreciate it," Mia said when she'd collected herself some. "You said your name was . . ."

"Lambert! Help me out here!" interrupted Lynlee with a yell from down the hall. "I keep reading a bad circuit on this panel, and I keep tripping the whole thing when I try to energize it."

Too curious not to follow Eli, they found Lynlee near a junction box, staring in frustration as a device in her hand registered her woes in red lights. Mia didn't pretend to understand the problem, although she could readily grasp it was recondite. However, it was also quickly solved, and within a few minutes, everything was in working order.

When Lynlee had finished thanking him, Eli turned to Mia and replied, "Sorry about that. Minor emergencies like this happen, although I thought we covered all these details before we took off."

Eli then shot a glance at Lynlee, who gave a guilty smile. "I know, I know. I'll do better next time."

"Why did Lynlee call you Lambert?" inserted Mia curiously.

"Oh, my bad," said Lynlee sheepishly. "Eli hates it when we call him that, but somewhere along the way we started calling him by his last name because we figured out it's the surest way to get his attention. If you haven't been introduced yet, Mia, Tyber, this is Eli, my lead and one of the Rail Drivers' field technicians. If you ever need something fixed, he's the person to call."

"Oh, that reminds me," said Eli, distractedly turning to Mia, "Tyber will probably need something more secure than what I worked out with him this time, and you sound really adamant about not keeping him in any kind of kennel, so—"

Eli was interrupted by a notification on his handheld link.

"It's like a curse, I swear," muttered Eli as he glanced at his tiny black tablet. "Apparently, I'm needed. At any rate, grab me sometime and we'll arrange something more permanent for him. It was nice meeting you, Mia."

Mia waved as Eli dashed off.

"Well, I'm glad we got that fixed quickly," said Lynlee as Eli disappeared around a corner. "Now, if I don't miss my guess, they're about to serve lunch. We should hurry there before the rush."

"Oh, that's right. I've still got to work out where I'm serving Tyber his chow," said Mia.

After some inquiries and planning on Tyber's behalf, Mia and Lynlee wasted no time before heading to the mess hall. The food the ship served was pleasant enough, and the crew ate fairly well for space travelers. Indeed, to Mia it was a considerable step up from what she'd grown used to. Lynlee was also excellent company for the duration, happy to answer Mia's questions. The mess hall was also where Mia made another key acquaintance, for as they sat down to eat, a figure no taller than Lynlee took the seat beside them. She wore an officer's hat, a sword that almost dragged along the floor, and a long coat. At first Mia thought she was another youth like Lynlee, or even a child playing dress-up, but was corrected not long after when Lynlee introduced her.

"Oh, Mia! I need to introduce you to Captain Rivkah Stratweiss, the *John Henry's* captain. She looks after our company's transportation needs."

Mia did a double take, then somewhat abashedly accepted the short captain's extended hand.

The ship captain smiled. "Ah, so this is the new trainer I've been hearing so much about. Pleased to make your acquaintance. I hope your time here will be long and fruitful."

"I'm a bit confused. I thought Jack Rikeman was the captain of the Rail Drivers," said Mia.

"He is. I'm the *ship* captain," said Rivkah. "It's an understandable mistake, but we're actually separate crews. The Rail Drivers pay us a retainer to lease part of the cargo hold and furnish them transport as the need arises. The *John Henry*, in turn, gleans a steady customer that doubles as ship security. It's a mutually beneficial relationship for both crews this way. A freighter this size is a money sink if left idle, so the ship crew remains separate, transporting cargo when the Rail Drivers are stationed for extended periods. It then serves as a base of operations for the mercs. My crew, in turn, gets a stable paying client to lease a portion of the *John Henry*'s cargo space.

"Not to mention they both benefit from the ability to float technicians like Eli and me between them," added Lynlee with a smile.

"That's true. The added manpower does save us a lot of time," said Rivkah with a smile. "I also occasionally enlist the Rail Drivers as a security detail, since guarded transport sometimes charges a better rate. Of course, the fact we're reputed to have them aboard as regulars tends to act as a deterrent in itself, since pirates avoid boarding anything that may fight back."

Mia enjoyed the conversation, and after determining eating arrangements for Tyber, she knew her next task was going to be exercise and her appointment with the ship's doctor. As she approached the sick bay, she heard a familiar voice call out, "Come on in, Mia."

Sure enough, Dr. Garnier was there to greet her inside.

"Now, I'm told your last physician had an accident that blew away most of your medical history, so I hope you don't mind if I give you a thorough examination for my records. I do this with most newcomers, and any details you can give me will be helpful. For starters, I'd like to have a look at those beautiful ear grafts of yours. I noticed you seem to have some healing still happening at your fingertips. Did something happen?"

"I actually wanted your opinion on them. As a doctor, do you think they're going to grow back okay?" asked Mia, trying not to tremble as she presented them.

Dr. Garnier grasped Mia's fingers tenderly and, after running a scanning device over them, said, "Based on these findings, they'll be fine once they grow back fully. They've been induced to regrow harder and with a stronger binding, but otherwise, they seem fairly normal. Just keep them clean and you'll probably have nails that are the envy of us all. I'm also getting signs of some genetic adjustment. Did you aim to have claws at some point, or was this more incidental to the other biografts?"

"It's a long story," said Mia with a shake of her head. "Let's just say I'm relieved to hear mine *won't* look like

Tyber's! What that deranged group thought they would accomplish when they did this to me, I'll never know."

Taking her seat, Mia tried to endure the examination with decorum as the physician shone a light in her eyes and replied, "I hope you don't mind if I marvel. I'm not generally into modifications like these, but I know good work when I see it, and whoever set you up with these did a marvelous job. Your tapetum lucidum is masterfully set. Your eyes react well, and you don't seem to have any vision problems. I bet you have excellent night vision. Now I'm going to feel the bases of your ears. Everything seems stable and in order there. Pants please. How well can you move your tail?"

"Oh, well enough," said Mia, letting herself stretch. "I'll be honest, I tend to stuff it down a pant leg most of the time right now. It knocks things over when it's out and keeps my pants lower than I'm comfortable with."

"Understandable, although you may still be throwing your center of balance off by doing so. If it's as well implemented as your ears, then you're probably better off modifying your wardrobe to accommodate it. It is a beautiful tail after all. You should enjoy it. I'm actually fascinated by the seamless movements your add-ons employ. The nerve binding must have been fine-tuned fantastically to make them all work so well. Do you mind sharing how you came by them?"

"*Megalodon*," said Mia self-consciously, "and I'd rather not talk about it if it's all right with you."

"I noticed you skirted the topic when I asked about the black labs earlier too. I'm going to go out on a limb and guess these grafts weren't a completely voluntary procedure."

Mia didn't respond. A moment later she felt a hand on her shoulder as the doctor said in a gentle tone, "I won't pry, but you should know there's an unspoken rule on this ship. Call it a superstition of mine, or maybe an occupational hazard. We all have secrets and things we'd as soon ignore or forget, but it's important that someone here knows the whole story. We can't very well cover each other's backs if we don't know there's a vulnerability. I've seen a lot of people get cornered or struck down because they couldn't trust someone to watch out for them. So with that in mind, I hope you'll find a way to share that story with somebody aboard. Naturally, I come with the added benefit of being your physician, so secret keeping comes with the territory, but I understand if you don't want to take me into your confidence."

"Do you have one, Dr. Garnier?" asked Mia after a moment. "A secret, I mean?"

"A few," said the doctor with a smile. "One is that I actually took on this role to *avoid* work on the battlefield. It's not that I'm squeamish about bloody scenes or wounded soldiers, but I've learned that I do get a bit panicky when there are bullets flying overhead. You should know most of the crew just calls me Valerie. Lynlee is the only one who calls me Doctor because I played pediatrician for war orphans like her not so long ago. I suppose she gave you the impression I was a full-fledged doctor, but I'm only a med tech."

"Why don't you just go into civilian medicine if you don't like the battlefield?" asked Mia, her curiosity piqued.

"I have my reasons. One is I prefer the opportunities this role gives me. The people it lets me help. People like Lynlee when she was little. Another is that while I love my occupation, I've discovered I can't stand medical culture. Too many supermen trying to be untouchable, and too afraid or proud to admit when they're mistaken."

"I see." Mia wanted to say more, but after a moment she merely replied, "I really appreciate this, Doctor, erm, Valerie, and I hope I can share my story with you soon. Please understand, I'm still getting used to a medic treating me well again."

"I understand," said Valerie with a sober nod, then heaving a deep breath, declared in a cheerier tone. "Well, if you need something to sleep or relax, just ask. This med tech doubles as a bartender, you know."

"I'll keep that in mind," said Mia with a laugh. With Mia's examination concluded, Mia walked back to her bunk room. The day had been plenty eventful, and as the time to wind down and turn in was upon them, Mia looked forward to a few quiet moments before rest. She'd only taken off her boots and grabbed her toothbrush when Tyber wandered in after, and this flustered Lynlee.

"Is Tyber supposed to be here with us?" she asked nervously.

Mia looked about, realizing she'd taken it for granted that Tyber would be staying nearby, and replied, "Well, I hoped he could. I realize he's not your everyday house cat, but I promise he won't bother anyone."

"But . . ." Lynlee stammered, then whispered to Mia, "isn't he a *boy* tiger?"

"Your point?" asked Mia.

"He's in the girl's sector. We change in here," said the teenager skittishly.

Mia smirked and, trying to curb her urge to tease, replied, "What? Are you worried he'll see something? You realize *he's* been naked this whole time and you haven't been worried."

"W-well, that's true," said Lynlee, blushing, "but he has fur."

"Oh, good grief! Watch," said Mia, and with that, stripped down where she stood to don her pajamas, much to Lynlee's alarm. Tyber, unsure of what exactly was going on, gave little more than a disinterested glance as he began to evaluate the room for a comfortable corner to curl up in.

"You see? It won't make any difference to him," said Mia when she had finished changing. "However, I'm sure if you asked, Tyber would look away for you because he's a gentleman."

"Look away? Why? I don't follow," asked Tyber, having listened but, as with much of what he could make no sense of, had only given the mildest attention.

"So you won't see us girls without clothes on," replied Mia flippantly.

"Yes, but why?" repeated Tyber, confused.

"Oh, never mind! I'll just change in the washroom," said Lynlee. She wouldn't speak again until they were all curled up in their bunks and Mia asked why Valerie wasn't joining them.

"Oh, sometimes Valerie stays up a while until Dr. Roche relieves her for the night shift. Sometimes she's asleep at the same time as the rest of us, and sometimes she's up all night. Watching her work is what convinced me I could never be a doctor. I swear doctors don't live like normal people!" murmured Lynlee, "So, what do you think of our crew so far?"

"I honestly had no idea what to expect when I came here," said Mia as she gently stroked Tyber, who purred gently as he slept beside her bunk. "But then I never expected to go into this line of work, and I'm still worried I'm going to panic when I see action."

"Oh, so you're planning to go in with him? I didn't realize you would both be in the field together! That explains why you had gear moved to the armory."

Lynlee eventually managed to quiet herself down to sleep. As her bunkmate slept, Mia turned over and sentimentally clasped the handgun Electra had given her in its holster. She then gave a soft sigh and let herself drift to sleep.

CHAPTER 7

Transit to Mission

The Rail Drivers stationed at Kiito Mining Base were only scheduled to be there a week or two, and Mia got the feeling many crew members were viewing it as something of a sabbatical, enjoying the local atmosphere and schedule when they weren't part of the patrols. Lynlee noted at several points she was looking forward to shopping there, even though she and Eli were subcontracted to help with some of the new wings.

As supplemental security, Mia was expected to look the part, even if all she was doing was effectively backing up station security guards. Lynlee was only too happy to help Mia get her equipment fitted with patches and tags bearing the Rail Driver Mercenary Company's trademark insignia, which looked like a railway spike being hammered into the ground with lightning bolts. To signal their association, Tyber would wear a customized harness with a matching insignia, which had been carefully crafted to fit him comfortably. There would be no saddle, for Mia and Tyber agreed from the start that while his agility had proven useful in tight pinches, he was no "steed" to be ridden.

Mia's patrols would only necessitate her handgun, allowing her to leave most of her other tools on the ship. More armaments were likely to be seen as excessive. Since Tyber's harness was designed to work like a bandolier with pouches and straps for gear, it would similarly remain empty. With such a light schedule, it left Rikeman free to teach her the ropes of her new work, and he warned her she'd spend much of her schedule memorizing the crew's regulations, as well as demonstrate and hone certain basic skills like gear maintenance and personal defense, among other things. While patrolling, she and Tyber were to follow the routes the security guards assigned and generally follow their commands. This was arguably her easiest task since the base actually seemed rather quiet compared to *Megalodon*, with fewer distractions to compete for her attention. Still, it was a whole different feeling trying to retain one's situational awareness in the presence of such stimulation instead of passively surrendering to the atmosphere as she might once have. After her first shift, she was to meet with Eli, who would take her to meet someone named Tim so she could get measured for her space suit.

Kiito Base was a pleasant site, with no shortage of bustle and its own eccentricities. Among the first things

Mia noted was that the whole facility looked a bit like an airport, with signs depicting arrivals alongside timetables. However, Mia learned the hard way these arrivals weren't for ships. In fact, when a ground-quaking crash occurred about the time one of these "arrivals" occurred, she'd nearly bumped into a security guard while running in the direction it had come from.

"Whoa, whoa! Where's the fire?" the security guard asked.

"Didn't you feel it? It sounded like an explosion, or at least a major crash! People could be hurt!" said Mia emphatically.

The security guard paused for a moment, then smiled as he shook his head and pointed to the schedule, "Oh! You mean the eight-twenty-three arrival just now."

"Arrival? You mean there are ships that are *supposed* to make that sound like that when they land!?" asked Mia in exasperation and disbelief.

"No, no. Those charts aren't for ship arrivals. They're *asteroid* arrivals," explained the security guard. "That's how Kiito Base works. Our crews crash asteroids from the nearby belt into this planetoid every day, then mine them out afterward."

"Oh," said Mia after a moment, palming her forehead with a mix of relief and embarrassment.

"I take it you're part of the Rail Driver crew we hired to help beef up security while we link up the new live-in sector?"

"Guilty as charged, though please don't hold it against them. I'm still new," said Mia. "I must look like an idiot."

"You don't have anything to be ashamed of," he said. "I've worked in this place for years, and I've seen every reaction to those impacts from abject denial to fetal positions. I've even fielded a few panic attacks. For someone who didn't know what was going on, you responded amazingly well. Now that you know what the schedule is, you'll know what to do. As you can see, the next big one is due about four and a half hours from now, and then one other lands before dark. The others will impact too far off to make much difference. Just find a good handhold when they land, since some arrivals are bumpier than others."

"They . . . predict these happenings?" asked Tyber.

"Sounds more like they schedule them if they're deliberately pushing these rocks into the planet themselves," murmured Mia with a shrug. "I guess I'll just have to warn you when they happen."

"Wow! The tiger talks!" said the officer with a slight shock as he stared down at Tyber.

"Yep. My partner talks," said Mia, patting Tyber. "Sorry for troubling you, sir. Hopefully, we won't cause you any more trouble."

This was just a sample of some of the interactions on board. People were kind and helpful and always interested in what Mia and Tyber were up to. Tyber seemed cognizant of the fact he was an icon, whether he wanted to be or not, and Mia noticed he would refrain from speech while they were in public, to the point where she sometimes had to guess what he wanted. He wouldn't tell her why he was doing this, but Mia guessed it was just his way of trying to curb people's excitement, and after the second day, it was clear she would need to ask for quieter routes to patrol.

Her interaction with the security guard had been short, but to Mia's embarrassment, it was far from the last time she would meet him, and it was when she came to see Rikeman at the end of the day that she encountered him again, talking to Rikeman outside the main loading dock.

"Oh, Mia, come meet Kiito mining complex's chief of security, Mr. Darek Carter. Mr. Carter, these are some of my newer recruits," said Rikeman as they walked up.

"No need. We've already met," said the guard with a smile.

Mia fumbled nervously as she realized the guard she'd bumped into was the security chief, and probably their client.

"Well, I hope you like them. They're that exotic unit your superiors were so excited about," said Rikeman.

"I do. I see a lot of promise in them. I just can't get them to understand you're all here to secure this base, not public relations," said the security chief before turning to address Mia. "Command keeps telling me how popular you and your tiger are. That's all well and good, but it's a mixed blessing for my officers, as you draw a bit of a crowd with the workforce and their families. I was just talking to Rikeman about moving you to some of the quieter sectors, or even to patrol the new wings while they're still off-limits to the public."

"Oh, that's actually a relief to hear," said Mia. "I'm not saying this isn't doable, but I agree that Tyber is drawing quite a lot of attention."

"Was there something you needed?" asked Rikeman.

"I wanted to ask about the next part of my schedule. I know you told me earlier I was meeting a guy named Tim, but now it says I'm supposed to meet Eli and a crewman named Nikki for something or other. Do you know what that's about?"

"Your suit fitting," said Rikeman, then gave a tut and clasped his forehead as he replied. "Oh, that's right! You haven't met Nikki yet! She's transferring her gear to the *John Henry* today. Head to the *John Henry's* berth and find Lynlee and Eli. You'll probably find them helping her unload her mech if they haven't already finished."

"On it. Let's go, Tyber," said Mia.

As the two left, Mia thought she could just barely hear the security chief say, "So where did you find those two? They seem like a fancy pair, even for you."

Rikeman didn't answer the chief right away, but discreetly watched as Mia turned a corner out of hearing range before he replied, "Someone brought them to me actually. How did they respond to the asteroid strike?"

"I thought they handled it pretty well."

"Did she do her homework and realize what was happening?"

"No, but what impressed me was they ran *toward* the danger when it happened," said the security chief. "They wanted to help and even stuck their necks out to do so. That's a hard quality to find. We can train people to spot trouble early, but it takes more than training to face trouble head-on instead of running away from it or pretending it's someone else's business. I think those two show a lot of promise."

"Is that so?" said Rikeman, putting his hand on his hip. "Well, maybe I took a better bet than I thought."

CHAPTER 8

Suited for the Job

Mia and Tyber entered the *John Henry*'s loading bay in time to see Mia and Eli torquing clamps onto the feet of a large mech as it stepped into a transport station.

"Mia! Just in time!" said Eli.

"Nikki, come on down and meet the two new recruits," called out Lynlee in response.

Mia looked up to see a driver emerge from the back of the mech, dressed in a black jacket over a vibrant red jumpsuit. Lynlee bounced up alongside to introduce Mia as she climbed down.

"Nikki, meet Mia, our new genetibeast trainer, and behind her is her partner, Tyber. Mia, Tyber, let me introduce you to Nikki Li. She's a member of the Raiden Alliance freedom fighters, who we work with from time to time. She's one of the best exobionic mech drivers you could ever hope to meet," said Lynlee with a proud grin as the driver strode up.

Mia had seen enough about people's stances to feel she could read them, and Nikki's stance was unmistakably anti-authoritarian. Her body language was open to the point of defiance. Her black jacket tempered the loud appearance that her bright red skin-tight jumpsuit evoked, and her hair appeared to be in its own form of rebellion. That said, Nikki's appearance wasn't unfriendly, and even had a gentle side to it. As Mia held out an accepting hand, Nikki shook it with only a mild hint of hesitation.

"The Raiden Alliance tends to loan Nikki and her mech out to us every so often in return for the occasional favor. It's a chance for her to make money for them, and we get access to a capable mech pilot, so it's a win-win," explained Eli.

"I'm afraid I'm as ignorant about mechs as it gets," said Mia apologetically as she addressed Nikki. "I had a date with a mech driver once. He told me all about his . . . I think he called it a 'raptor' or something. It was boring."

"Oh, a Raptr-2250. Let me guess, boundless praise?" replied Nikki with a mildly sarcastic trenchancy.

Mia smirked and said, "Sort of, although I think he likened driving one to 'a deep tissue massage from a gorilla.'"

"Ha-ha, I believe it!" said Nikki with a slow nod. "Sounds like you got him to really open up to you then. Yeah, those ship-to-ship boarding models aren't known for their comfort. Don't broadcast this, but frankly I find their drivers intolerable. So you're the new recruit with the tiger. Is he all right?"

Mia turned to see Tyber pacing around Nikki's mech, staring in bafflement, and it only slowly dawned on her that Tyber had never seen a mech before.

"What is it?" asked Tyber after a moment.

"That, my striped friend, is a Kitsun TAG 19! One of the most agile mecha in its size class, packing a variable payload for anti-infantry or armored assault and an arm-mounted rapid-fire mass driver," said Nikki proudly.

"People . . . use these?" asked Tyber.

"That's right. People drive them, sort of like the ships and land vehicles," said Mia, then turned. "Lynlee, would you be all right watching Tyber for an hour while I'm gone? I'd rather not subject him to two shuttle rides just so he can watch me get a fitting for something he'll never use."

"Oh, talk me into it," said Lynlee with facetious glee as she grinned from ear to ear.

"This is a formidable predator," said Tyber, once more choosing his words carefully as he spoke. "Are they common?"

"Well, if I can impress the tiger, then my day is made," said Nikki with a self-satisfied smirk as she musingly watched Tyber ponder the vehicle. "I don't know what you'd call common, but I'd hardly call mechs a rare sight."

"I think he's feeling a little intimidated," said Lynlee as she came alongside and stroked Tyber. Tyber didn't respond, except by snorting dismissively and feigning disinterest. However, Mia could read between the lines. Tyber was an apex predator, and the idea of something big and strong enough to merit his caution had to test the bounds of his understanding and was more than a little disruptive to his self-perception.

"Well, I'm satisfied we've got *Silver* strapped in sufficiently for transport," announced Eli. "Lynlee, we'll be back in a little bit once we've had our suits checked."

"Have fun. Tyber and I will be here when you get back," said Lynlee.

Boarding an in-base trainway, they shuttled to a section of the base that appeared to be some kind of repurposed mining and excavation repair shop. Inside was an array of small craft and machines. Eli cautioned Mia to stay close to him and Nikki, and she obliged but privately found the notion humorous, as the facility had nothing on the dives she'd visited as a space nomad. She'd already patrolled with Tyber, and what few figures on Kiito did raise her suspicions so far had all kept their distance. If anything, she worried she was standing out, as her biografts, however pleasant, came with their own connotations. She'd marveled on several occasions how rosy-tinted her opinion of biografts had been before she'd obtained the ones she now had. It was not until they had become a permanent feature that she grasped their mixed nature, for regardless of quality or intent, they were the marks of a major investment in nonconformity and shock value for its own sake, and nothing would change that. She'd already noticed a change in the nature and demographics of the attention she drew, and it wasn't an altogether welcome one.

The tunneled-out refuge felt haphazardly built, and Mia had a feeling based on their uneven strides that the gravity well projection system was on the fritz. The shop, like the process itself, was straightforward and clean. In retrospect, it even seemed relatively uneventful. Mia gathered from Eli's comments that Tim was formerly another technician of the Rail Driver Company but had chosen this work over maintenance. He'd been expecting the three of them and wasted no time in showing Mia what he'd prepared in anticipation of their arrival.

"Is that what it's supposed to look like on me?" Mia asked when she first laid eyes on the digital rendering of the design.

"Not bad. Looks like you even made some concessions for her fancy biografts," commented Nikki.

"Miss Garnier sent me the measurements when Rikeman made the order for you. It's simply a standard agility model like the one Eli's wearing," said Tim, glancing at his fellow technician.

Mia glanced at Eli and did a double take, wondering how she hadn't noticed it before. Indeed, under his jacket and coveralls, Eli had a contiguous layer of dark gray clothing with hazard color highlights in key places, and as she looked, she realized it bore a striking resemblance to the skintight jumpsuit Nikki was wearing.

"Wait, *that's* a space suit under there?" she asked Eli.

"And one of mine at that," said Tim as he walked around Eli and Nikki like they were modeling for him as he elaborated. "It works by constricting to the form of the wearer, so it won't balloon up in space. The material can even go under your normal clothes as Eli has them now, provided you leave room to access the controls. Some pilots and technicians wear their suits constantly as a precaution, only removing it for cleaning or maintenance. The main drawback is they can't adapt to any major changes to body shape, so they're essentially nontransferable, unless you're the exact same height and build.

"Congratulations, now we're all obligated to maintain our girlish figures," said Eli flippantly.

Mia gave a wry smile and rolled her eyes at this remark.

"Very funny. But seriously, hear me out here! Wouldn't a suit like this be kind of . . . unusual?" asked Mia with a tilt of her head. "I mean, I've read about these, and I'm told they make a space walk go from a chore to a treat, but shouldn't a combat space suit be a little more . . . protective?"

"The idea is to preserve your dexterity," said Tim. "Space combat is possibly the most unforgiving theater of warfare yet. The vacuum of space makes it so any hit that breaches the suit and isn't closed completely in a matter of seconds is lethal. Now, for mech drivers like Nikki, the requirements are a little different. You can see by the wear in the saddle area, she uses it inside her mech more than in space. I recommend these despite their cost and single-user limitations because they minimize both your silhouette and reaction time. You wear one of these, and in a boarding scenario, you'll be able to act faster than your enemy . . . hopefully."

"If you want added protection, you can also wear your body armor over it," added Nikki.

"And I recommend you do so if it comes to that," said Tim fervently. "Ship boarding is not a scenario to be taken lightly."

Mia appreciated the input, and as their conversation continued, Tim examined Eli's and Nikki's suits for wear points to ensure they were still in top working order. Mia learned Nikki and Eli were among his more regular customers since they tended to use their suits more extensively. As a technician, Eli was often out on the skin of the ship fixing things for Captain Stratweiss, but Mia had to ask about Nikki's reason for the added features on her suit.

"In my case, it's the spine guard I need most for when I drive my mech," explained Nikki. "That fancy fabric that expands and contracts can be made tension reactive, and when connected to my helmet, it can stiffen in response to unnatural spikes in motion and pressure, which reduces the impact on my body while driving my mech. It ensures I don't break my neck jumping around in a machine three times my size. The redundant layer of life support helps too."

"So it's like safety gear as well as a space suit," said Mia. "The more I hear about this, the more I'm looking forward to it. I'm nervous to ask how much this is gonna cost, as it sounds expensive."

"Rikeman won't gouge you for this. You might have to pay for it over the course of a few contracts, but since this is standard gear for the job, Rikeman never quibbles about financing it for people," Tim assured her as he wrote down notes on an adjustment or two for Mia's biografts. "I admit this is the first time I've installed a tail placement, but I am familiar with the principle, and based on what I know, this ought to work for you without a hitch."

"Actually, can we skip the tail?" asked Mia. "I mean, that may sound stupid, but—"

"No! That's actually what I'd prefer!" said Tim emphatically. "Bear in mind, you may need to don this suit in seconds while the whole ship is shaking, and most of the time spent donning these is sliding the appendages into place. If you are willing to endure going without, I would highly suggest simply stuffing your biograft down a leg or into the small of your back, as it should still conform to you fairly well without incident. If when you come back in a couple weeks you find it isn't to your liking, we can easily add an accommodation for it post-fitting."

"Wait? Aren't we leaving in a few days on the *John Henry* for our next mission!?" asked Mia as she glanced up at Nikki.

"Relax. Someone will fly you back here to let you try it on when the time comes," said Nikki. "Probably Lambert. This boy scout is always getting talked into favors."

"Thanks," said Eli hesitantly.

Mia watched as Tim did a quick inspection of Nikki's and Eli's suits, then ran a handful of checks on them. Like clockwork, Eli felt his handheld communicator calling and was soon dispatched, so he had to leave to help the base staff negotiate with some airlock framers.

"Poor guy hasn't caught a break in five years," said Nikki, shaking her head. "Come on. I'll buy you a drink before we head back."

Mia accepted, and a few minutes later, they were sitting with drinks at an establishment Nikki knew of.

"So, a genetibeast trainer. They never told us about *that* occupation on career day," said Nikki as she nursed what advertised itself to be a coffee blend of some kind. "Then again, growing up in Singularity Dawn, most jobs had to be tinted in terms of how they would contribute to our *glorious nation's* power base." She rolled her eyes before glancing back at Mia.

Mia hid behind her own glass and made a self-conscious grin behind it as she shrugged and replied, "Yeah, well, I'm actually very new to the whole trainer thing. The truth is the only reason I was allowed to take care of Tyber is because he trusts me. If he didn't, I'm not sure there'd be a way anyone could handle him."

"He does seem pretty fond of you," said Nikki. "You know, with a genetibeast like that, you'd pass as a pretty convincing agent of Singularity Dawn. The kind to send in to spy on potential enemies of the state."

Mia smirked as if she'd heard a joke, but as she saw Nikki's expression, she sobered up and asked in horror, "Wait, are you really worried I'm some kind of spy for the SD?"

"Maybe. That genetibeast of yours does remind me a lot of the White Tiger of the West in Chinese astrology. Given Singularity Dawn prides itself on having roots in Eastern tradition, it would fit that would be the kind of creature they'd breed for an operative. So, convince me otherwise," challenged Nikki with a relaxed sip.

Mia sputtered. Of course, what Nikki was suggesting was not the case, but the longer she thought about it, the more she understood where Nikki's misgivings originated. Singularity Dawn was, without question, a tyrannical nation, known throughout the sector for its aggressive mandate of expansion, its iron-fisted rule, oppressive surveillance-state mentality, and propensity for disintegration warfare. Indeed, their attitudes toward other nations seldom changed in any meaningful way, and they often sued for peace only as a facade to more subtly undermine their opposition. It was a subject Mia never liked to dwell on, but she knew enough to know they had fanatical operatives who would go to reckless lengths to put the hurt on perceived "enemies" of the state. Even a few crime lords on *Megalodon* had paid that price before.

Mia's mind raced for a reassuring answer, but as she thought about it, she said with reluctance, "I don't think I really have any good way to convince you. Honestly, the more I think about it, the more I realize you probably have many reasons to be suspicious of me. But I can assure you I'm not your enemy. I know that doesn't help a lot right now, but I hope Tyber and I can prove that to you in our coming mission together."

Nikki stared Mia down for a while before slowly replying, "Good response. Honest, factual, and light on the sappy sentiment. You're right. I do have a lot of reasons to watch you closely. I just wanted you to know why I'm doing so. I suppose we'll both have to see what happens."

Nikki leaned forward then and added, "Of course, it helps that you're wearing this and not a subdermal implant." Nikki pointed to Mia's wrist display. "I've never seen a Singularity Dawn agent who would wear one, and if it's a fake, it's the best I've seen yet, as it behaves just like the real thing around my mech, *Silver*. It isn't widely advertised, but the Raiden Alliance uses Philos technology to repel SD's ciphers and hackers. It came with Altaire's weapons when they armed us for rebellion. I don't really trust Philos either, but it's still our best countermeasure to the Singularity Dawn's information warfare, and even *Silver's* firmware is predominantly of Philos architecture and code. Without it, even Caladria could hack our systems, so we've kind of been dependent on it from day one. Do you trust Philos?"

"More than what?" asked Mia tactfully.

Nikki smiled, "Well put. Yeah, I sometimes think Philos must find people like me and the Raiden Alliance a handy pretext. A way to disrupt Singularity Dawn's data infrastructure. Still, I can't say that sits badly with me. Singularity Dawn has never been able to counter

Philosophia completely, short of adding blind spots to their surveillance-state infrastructure, and in that sense they've done more for our rebellion than anyone else. Not even their 'Ascension Network' can really compete with it. No, the fact is Singularity Dawn fears the AI. They see it as a poison with the potential to infect and unseat them from their places of power. Some of my comrades see that as salvation. Others view it as merely trading one overlord for another, but at least we know they're opposed to each other."

"Sounds like we have very similar opinions of Philos," said Mia, glancing down at her wrist display. "I generally like it, but sometimes it scares me what it can do, but for better or for worse, it's my best option right now."

"Was Philos who sent you?" asked Nikki spontaneously.

"No!" Mia paused, considering, and then said in a lower tone, "At least, that's not how I see it."

Nikki nodded in acknowledgment and, as if reaching a consensus they'd said enough between them, stood to go. Nikki's words had given Mia plenty of food for thought and had cast the whole idea of keeping secrets in a new light. It was becoming apparent everyone on the *John Henry* had a past, and Valerie had been astute in observing that secrets came with the territory. Perhaps it had come as a mercy that night, when the four girls had finished bedding down, that Lynlee asked the dreaded question.

"Hey, Mia, you mentioned black labs at one point. Is Tyber some kind of rescue from there?" Lynlee asked. "I've heard of the Global Union seizing illegally engineered beasts from the black market and pairing the more stable ones with special caretakers to ensure they have good homes. Is that what happened?"

Mia could sense Nikki shifting in her bunk to prop herself on an elbow, clearly interested by the remark.

"Lin-lin, cut her some slack," said Valerie from her own bunk. "Not everyone wants to tell you their life story."

Mia could see the medic was working hard to deflect the subject for her, and appreciated the gesture, but knew it to be unnecessary.

"Oh, I'd say I'm the one who got rescued," chortled Mia with a stretch. "I'd be a very sad footnote apart from Tyber."

"Not so. Neither of us would be free if we hadn't worked together," said Tyber, speaking up.

"Sounds like quite a story," said Lynlee, leaning her head over the bunk above. "What happened?"

"Well, understand it's not a story I like telling often. Suffice to say, Tyber and I have each done some rescuing for the other," said Mia, pulling her covers close.

Carefully, she recounted her time in the black labs. Of the experimentation, of Tyber, and their impromptu escape, carefully leaving out Electra and Aster's role in it. It proved surprisingly easy to tell, although much briefer than she expected without their involvement. Lynlee listened like a child hearing a campfire story, and Nikki and Valerie kept a quiet gaze as they listened. Mia wrapped the story up by merely saying she obtained passage on a ship and from there was directed to Mr. Wilson of Philos, who then pulled some favors to help her stay with Tyber, and left it at that.

"I guess you and Tyber really are partners then," said Nikki when Mia had finished her story. "I'd guessed your relationship was more than just that of beast and trainer, but it's gratifying to have some context for it now."

"Would you rather this tale didn't leave the bunk-room?" asked Valerie delicately when she had finished.

"Oh, I'm not worried about that. Feel free to share it with whoever you like," said Mia. "It's just not a story I'm all that comfortable telling yet. I'm leaving parts out, and I may never be able to tell the whole story. I'm a little surprised I was able to tell you all this much."

"Mia, if your story is even remotely like you say, then you'll do just fine. I would go so far as to say you and Tyber will be some of the strongest additions this crew has had in a while," said Nikki, then added with a yawn, "I'd gladly recruit you for the Raiden Alliance if you weren't already part of this outfit."

Mia appreciated the vote of confidence, especially given what Nikki had said before. As everyone quieted down, she turned over, sentimentally clasping the handgun in its holster as before, and let herself drift to sleep.

CHAPTER 9

Journey to Zengin III

"**L**ook, I know that accountant had his reasons for giving you only the Cliff Notes, but for pity's sake, you could have warned me the girl had severe trauma involving medicos!" exclaimed Valerie.

"You know, I never would have pictured them for lab escapees," said Jack, stroking his mustache. "That explains why the tiger is so shrewd. Even Altaire's elite K-9 units don't get that kind of intellect."

"Are you even listening to me?" asked Valerie.

"Look, I wasn't given the details. I know as well as you do that our Philos contact isn't the most forthcoming, but the man's never done wrong by us as a client. All he said was that she was a former space nomad taking care of a genetibeast rescue with extraordinary combat capabilities, and assured me that she had legal authority to care for him. I checked into her, and she isn't wanted anywhere, at least not officially, and has shown she has the right attitude and the will to pull her own weight. Beyond that, it's up to her to share, not us."

"So you didn't know what happened to her on the megaship?"

"I didn't, and I had no plans to find out," said Jack bluntly. "Our line of work demands it. Take sergeant 'Evski. When he joined, he came from the highlands of Caladria with scars of every kind and in every place. To this day, he beds down in a locked space the size of a broom closet. He does it because he's been known to strangle passersby in his sleep. It's how he's wired to protect himself, and he's never shared what made him that way. Despite his personal demons, he's a good man and one of our toughest line troops. I may even have him shadow Mia for the contract coming up on Zengin III."

"I know that. It's just . . ." Valerie paused, then said with a sigh, "I might have presented myself differently if I'd known."

"Did she run screaming from the sick bay?" asked Jack gruffly.

"No," muttered Valerie. "She put on a strong face, as I'd expect from any spacefarer."

"Then you did fine. Dr. Roche picked you as his assistant because you're hardworking, knowledgeable, and have a better bedside manner than he ever did. Now quit borrowing trouble. It's bad for your complexion."

In another part of the ship, Mia sat with several of her weapons and tools while her roommates enjoyed their downtime. She was overdue to familiarize herself with some of her gear, and she hoped her ignorance wasn't showing as she looked different pieces over. Electra had been diligent in explaining the industry and tactics of mercenary work in the field but had only given her the briefest notes on the equipment itself. Above her, Lynlee lounged in her bunk, enamored by Mia's optic camouflage. As Lynlee thumbed through the tech manual, Mia experimented with the color-shifting fabric.

"Eagle mod! This is fantastic! I don't know if it'll quite extend to Tyber, but it'll definitely hide *you* well enough, Mia! I'm amazed how smoothly the liquid image projection operates! According to the manual, it composites data of your surroundings to give you apt coloration when it can't keep up with your movements or has to enter an unexpected shutdown."

"Lynlee, use small, dumb-down talk for me. I flunked out at tech school," said Mia.

Lynlee rolled her eyes and grinned. "This cloak still turns the colors of your surroundings even if it can't make you invisible for some reason. It even obstructs you from satellites fairly effectively, and that's not easy to do anymore!" explained the teenage technician

"The person who gave it to me was pretty excited about its performance too. I'm a little sad I've yet to really use it," said Mia as she put on her headgear and briefly looked about. She noted the heads-up display, which seemed to mark the presence of something specific in her luggage, but Nikki's voice drew her attention away before she could find out more.

Nikki, who up to this point had been watching an exobionic mech sporting event on a tablet screen, glanced over as Mia had been looking about. She turned to sit up in her bunk and commented, "You're still unpacking some of this stuff? I thought you would have done this in the first week."

"This has been my first real opportunity," said Mia shyly. "I've been playing catch-up to learn our crew's rules, not to mention the *John Henry's* emergency systems. You know—fire suppression, shelter rooms, airlocks, the bulkhead layout. Things you're supposed to know on any ship you're going to stay on."

"You actually bothered to memorize those things?" asked Nikki.

"It's no joke!" said Mia, looking up with a stern expression. "Even if you're in a room with a tiny hull breach, you're still just as much of a goner. I've lived on starships my whole life, and if there's one thing space nomads try to pound on, it's that the vacuum of space is not to be taken lightly!"

"I'm not criticizing, I'm impressed, okay? Most people don't take it seriously enough," said Nikki, trying to change the subject. "Anyway, you're certainly packing some cutting-edge tools. Tension-reactive ceramic microplate armor, a Global Union–style military carbine, ghost SMGs, Philos-brand multispectral vision. Are you sure you didn't want to retire to a small estate instead?"

"Like I said, Wilson pulled some favors for me. I guess he wanted to make sure I got the best start I could," commented Mia, trying to steer past the fact that the gear had been obtained because she'd chosen to stay with Tyber.

"I must schmooze with the wrong people," murmured Nikki, reclining.

"It's nice. Still, I'm a bit nervous. Tyber and I still have several matters we need to address about our game plan once we're in the field," said Mia.

"Really? Like what?" asked Nikki.

"Well, upon learning I could communicate at range via the transceiver we made for his ear, Tyber started suggesting I do the instructing from somewhere more remote. I've tried to explain that I'm supposed to stay close by to, well, *handle* him, or at least pretend to for the sake of anyone watching. I'm well aware he could probably carry out any number of tasks alone, but I can't stand the idea of sending him into danger without being there to support him."

"M'lady, your ability to aid and instruct is not in question," asserted Tyber from his corner of the room, "but with all due respect, you are quite fragile."

"That's so mean, Tyber!" said Lynlee, sitting up in her bunk. "She's your partner, isn't she?"

"He's an eight-hundred-pound super-tiger, Lynlee," said Nikki with a stretch. "We're *all* fragile compared to him! He's just concerned about her welfare. I actually find it rather sweet you want to keep each other safe. I take it you've already brought this up with Captain Rikeman. What was his verdict?"

"Well, he seemed to appreciate the problem but hasn't said anything decisive about it yet," said Mia with a slight sigh. She knew Tyber's strengths stood in stark contrast to her own, but her concerns weren't just for Tyber's welfare. She'd meant what she said about wanting to be strong like Electra, and she wasn't going to attain that if she stayed on the sidelines.

"Just follow his orders and listen carefully for now. He doesn't always say it, but I've never seen Rikeman without a plan or at least a good grasp of the situation. Don't tell him I said this, but I feel he knows how to utilize me even better than the Raiden Alliance," said Nikki. "It's part of why I like to volunteer to work with the Rail Drivers."

"Say, have you shown any of your tools to Lambert yet?" asked Lynlee suddenly.

"Eli? No. Why do you ask?" replied Mia, glancing up at her bunkmate.

"Because Lambi's one of the best tinkerers on board," said Lynlee as she jumped down. "You give him half an hour with this stuff, and it'll be truly eagle mod when he's finished!"

"You keep using that word. What does that even mean, *eagle mod*?" asked Nikki.

"*I* can answer that," said Mia with grin. "It's shorthand for 'illegally modified.' The original term was *egal modied*. Post-American colonists like my grandparents used it as a way to talk about smuggled goods or back-channel services when they were railing against the corrupt litigation of Earth govs, you know, back in the days before the last homeworld war. It refers to something so great it can't be completely legal to do or have."

"Oh, that makes so much sense," said Nikki. "Well, that definitely marches to Lambert's beat. Take that handgun of his. I'm pretty sure that one breaks several Global Union statutes."

Lynlee started placing Mia's things in a crate and chimed, "Let's bring them over to him now. At the very least, he can do a systems check for you and get you familiar with them. I'd do it for you myself, but that isn't quite my field. Not yet anyway."

They traversed the engineering section, and Mia found herself enjoying the ambient hum of the engines.

She hadn't heard such sounds while she trained, and now that she was aboard the *John Henry*, she found them familiar and surprisingly reassuring. The *John Henry* was a clean but age-worn ship, with signs that it had more than a few stories to tell, and to Mia, this came as a comfort.

"What makes you so sure he'll have time to help tweak out my gear?" asked Mia skeptically as they walked.

"Eli has a personal rule. He'll drop almost any task to help you, provided you bother to ask for it in person and not over his handheld communicator."

"So is that why his contact info still hasn't synced up with mine?" asked Mia, looking down at her wrist display, "These generally sync automatically, or at least inform you if the other person has maxed out their privacy settings, but I've bumped into Eli several times now and haven't seen a trace of his digital aura."

"And you won't," said Lynlee plainly. "For the most part he doesn't have one."

"How's that even possible? Is he some kind of technophobe?" asked Mia.

Lynlee glanced back quizzically and, holding Mia's tools a little higher, said, "We're taking him these, and you're asking me if he's tech shy? Far from it! He just avoids leaving that kind of trail. 'Digital BO,' he calls it."

As they walked, Mia continued fidgeting with her wrist display and commanded it to show her own contact data. She smiled as her "opssistant" pulled up the information. Short for "operational assistant," most data carrying personal displays had them, and they were often portrayed in the form of a dolled-up person or creature, and to Mia's delight, hers had been made to resemble Aster down to its silvery eyes and ballerina-like grace. She suspected the real Aster was responsible for this, and she appreciated the comforting gesture.

"Cute chibi opssistant," said Eli, appearing out of the corner of Mia's eye. Mia's tail stood on end for a moment as she whirled about to face him.

"Oh, there you are, Eli," said Lynlee cheerfully.

Eli didn't respond to Lynlee, instead staring hard at Mia's display. He waved to the figure, which waved back politely, before pointing to his pocket as if making a request. Smiling, Eli pulled out his handheld display and manually synchronized it. "Aster hasn't lost her touch, has she?" Eli said. "Even as an opssistant, she's hard to say no to."

"Yeah," said Mia. Then the realization set in that Eli had used Aster's name. She glanced at Eli, who met her gaze briefly. He'd used the name deliberately, however subtly. Mia found herself flustered. Her ears had perked forward at the name and, upon becoming aware her features were tipping her hand, fought the urge to defensively turn her ears away again as she pondered the implications. Was he dropping some kind of hint? Or was he perhaps fishing for information? Unsure what else to do, she tried to formulate a good question to reply with in turn.

"Oh, that *is* cute!" said Lynlee obliviously as she pulled Mia's wrist aside to see the little figure. "She looks like an independently programmed avatar too! Eagle mod! Her reactions are so distinct! Did someone from *Megalodon* program it for you?"

"No. Just a friend from abroad." Mia looked back at Eli and asked, "How did you—"

"Sorry I left you waiting on that for so long," interrupted Eli. "Believe it or not, I've been meaning to sync my display with yours since you first arrived. I know this will sound odd, but I always input contact data to my handheld manually. That's what you were here to see me about, right? The syncing of my comms link to yours?"

"That and tweaking out Mia's new toys," said Lynlee, holding up the box.

Eli stepped over and looked inside before taking the box. "Not a bad assortment. Looks like you have some gear that can network too. That comes with its own risks, but they wouldn't make them if there weren't benefits too. Let's head to my workshop, where we can discuss this more thoroughly."

A few minutes later, the three of them were crammed into Eli's nook of a workstation. Eli began setting each item out for individual evaluation. Tyber peeked his head between the two girls as they stood just inside the entrance, listening silently. Mia stewed quietly, as she wanted to ask Eli about his earlier comment but felt unable to with Lynlee present.

"It's really quite sophisticated stuff," said Eli. "In fact, I don't think I can make a lot of improvements on these. First order of business is getting this visor of yours set up. Just try not to get too reliant on this thing. It's good hardware, but like your wrist display, it's vulnerable to signal-based attacks. I have some special firmware that will let you sever your connection when you reset it, but it's not guaranteed to work."

"How about plasmatic chambering for this?" asked Lynlee, motioning to Mia's firearms.

"Plas-what? What kind of modification is that?" asked Mia.

"You know, the addition of a plasma chamber on the barrel to ionize the bullet's surface and let it sear through kinetic armors before they can absorb any of the force," said Lynlee matter-of-factly.

"Better simplify that for Mia, Lynlee. I know what you're talking about, and *I* barely understood what you said," replied Eli.

"It's the only thing that can pierce certain armors. Is that *dumbed-down* enough for you both?" said Lynlee impertinently.

Eli pulled his own handgun from its holster and set it in front of Mia for reference. "Essentially, you're making an extra-hot tracer round. By inducing a delayed fusion reaction in the phosphorus on the surface of the bullet, it exits the chamber on the front of the barrel with searing qualities. It boosts even a low-caliber bullet's piercing power to contend with most personal armor, including armsuits. It's a modification I do for a lot of people."

"Wait, isn't that the modification Nikki was talking about? The one that goes against several GU statutes?" asked Mia.

"Well, you can't carry this into town, but then, who wants to carry one of these on a shopping trip?" said Eli somewhat abashedly. "Everybody complains about following the rules, but at the end of the day, weapon laws only disarm the law-abiding. Lynlee was asking about this gun specifically because she knows I could probably replace your IFF trigger-disabling system with one, and—"

"Wait, trigger disabling?" interrupted Mia, her eyes narrowing. "Like something external could keep my guns from firing?"

"On this model, essentially," said Eli. "It's easy enough to disable, but—"

"Get rid of it! Get rid of it now, and I don't mean just turn it off. I mean run a soldering pen through the chip! Make sure it can never be *re-enabled* again!"

"I think she wants one of your eagle mods," said Lynlee with a giggle.

"I think she does too," said Eli with a grin. "Oh, and I saw your stealth cloak in there too. Will this be your first time using optic camouflage?"

"I know how to use it, if that's what you're asking. Even without it, Tyber and I can be pretty sneaky when we want to be," said Mia proudly, hearkening back to her training.

Tyber recognized the term from earlier and nudged Mia. Glancing at the armor, he asked, "This optical covering . . . Lynlee spoke of it as well. What makes it so useful?"

"It makes me harder to see, Tyber. Weren't you listening earlier?" said Mia.

"Yes, but to what end? I don't sense it impedes tracking by scent, and I can hear your breath by the time scent becomes too imprecise. Sight is irrelevant."

"It works because humans have a lousy sense of smell, Tyber," said Eli with a grin. "My nose couldn't tell Lynlee from Mia here unless they at least used different shampoos, and I'd still have to get uncomfortably close to tell even then. We depend a lot on our vision to iden-tify things. By making her harder to see, most of your enemies will have a harder time finding or targeting you."

"I see," said Tyber after a moment. "I never thought of it like that. I'm not sure I quite understand how, but if this outfit hides you so well from humans, and I can successfully stalk prey with you at my side, then with some practice, we ought to do well."

At the word *practice*, Mia's tail stood on end. She moved to get up, cursing and bumping her head on an overhanging shelf as she did.

"Oh blast! I forgot I'm due to spar in the loading bay! Jack wants to see how well I can hold my own in hand-to-hand. I gotta run!"

Eli stood with his current project and followed casually as Mia sped back up the engineering corridor and raced to the loading bay. He arrived a few minutes later to find Mia sparring her hardest on the mat with Jack. Taking a seat on a nearby crate beside Lynlee, he watched Mia spar with interest while idly continuing his work on the gear.

"Good height on your kicks. You're pretty limber for a tenderfoot," said Jack as they sparred.

"Thanks," said Mia. "I ended up turning stretching into an art when I was in the black labs. Does it really show that I'm so new to this?"

"Being green and being unskilled are two different things," said Jack. "I can tell whoever taught you wanted to give you a solid foundation to work from. Your practice routine is well rounded, and you seem to have gotten yourself into decent shape for this. However, some things just come with exposure. Now, watch your right side, and remember to put your whole body into those kicks!"

Mia tried to follow the instruction but felt frustratingly outmatched by Jack's sheer stock and size, which bothered her. Rikeman was a tough figure, and Electra had cautioned her she'd often be up against things bigger and stronger than herself, but it was still vexing. How was she going to hold up if she encountered a real soldier like him in the battlefield?

"Not bad, although if I'm to get a proper feel for your skills, I should probably evaluate you against someone your own size. Let's have Lambert spar with you next," said Jack. He glanced at Eli. "He's about your size and weight. He should make a good sparring partner for you."

Mia turned to look at Eli, who looked up at them nervously.

"Jack, I'm a technician, not a martial artist," objected Eli. "Besides, you know my form is lousy."

"The way I see it, that makes you the ideal match," said Jack, cracking a grin. "You haven't practiced enough, and she hasn't been at it as long."

Eli sighed and, resigning himself, geared up and took his place across from Mia. They began, and the match took Mia a little by surprise. The heavy strikes she'd been throwing her whole body into weren't landing on Eli like they were on Jack. Rather, he evaded more than

Jack did, disrupting her broader strikes with smaller jabs and kicks before she could complete them. A moment later Eli nearly had her pinned to the ground. Yet before this decisive move was complete, a lurch from the *John Henry* caused Eli to look up, loosening his hold on her, and Mia used the opening to slip free. In one fluid move, she whirled behind him and slammed the technician into the mat, pinning him to the floor.

"Bravo!" said Lynlee as Mia finished the match.

"Yep. Definitely a space nomad," commented Jack. "Looks like you've had to navigate a scrap or two."

"A few," said Mia, helping Eli up. "Still, kind of a bum move for practice. Are you all right?"

"Serves me right for not stretching first," grumbled Eli, rotating his shoulder to relieve the soreness. "Yeah, I'm all right. Well played."

"What had you distracted?" asked Mia.

"He heard our slip drive go offline as we came out of slip space. You felt it too, didn't you, Lynlee?" commented Jack.

"Yeah," sighed Lynlee. "I guess we better go get it fixed. Captain Stratweiss will almost certainly want it working before we start unloading."

"Is something wrong with the ship?" asked Mia in concern.

"Nothing serious," said Eli. "Every so often, the *John Henry*'s slip drive goes offline when we exit slipspace. It doesn't harm us any, but we have to get it reset before we can use it again. Chief Engineer Shepherd has been trying to track the problem down for a while. Also, I finished work on your visor. That said, you might want to leave your goggles with the ship for this mission so they don't get sandblasted. I'll aim to be back in time to help you load Tyber's harness too."

Mia appreciated the gesture. As Eli left, Mia turned briefly to Jack and quizzically asked, "He was being figurative when he said 'sandblasted,' right?"

CHAPTER 10

Silver

Mia thought she'd get to lounge for a bit before landing, but upon returning to her room, she heard Nikki climb down from her bunk and ask, "Hey, Mia, can I borrow you for a bit? I need someone to lend me a hand putting the weather covers on my mech."

Mia followed, curious more than anything. As they entered the loading bay, Mia found herself reexamining Nikki's mech with interest. The mech itself was well over two times Mia's height, painted in a striking race-car red. It had, on its surface, an array of icons and symbols denoting components and safeties, as well as its name in chrome, along with a decal Mia hadn't noticed before. Set on the arm, it read in sharp letters NO MATTER THE ODDS!

Cognizant of Mia's gaze, Nikki walked up and patted her mech lovingly, "Yep, it's a beauty. Help me get its pajamas on!"

Mia glanced at the red mech's name and asked hesitantly, "This mech is called *Silver*?"

"Yeah," affirmed Nikki with a tone of confusion at the question. "That's the name. Didn't you see me securing it with Lambert and Lynlee earlier?"

"But it's red," noted Mia.

"Of course it's red!" fired back Nikki. "Just because I named it *Silver* doesn't mean I have to make it a certain color! There are other contexts, like 'Hi Ho Silver' and 'Long John Silver,' or even 'Quicksilver,' if that's your thing. Why does everyone get so hung up on the color?"

"How tall is it?" asked Mia, trying to tactfully change topics as she helped Nikki heave the padded tarp over the mech's shoulder.

"Thirteen feet, nine inches. Any bigger and *Silver* couldn't react fast enough to do what it's good at. I'm technically at a disadvantage against armsuits at this size," said Nikki.

"What's the difference between an armsuit and a mech anyway?" asked Mia as they climbed on top of *Silver* and pulled the covers over its shoulders.

Nikki nearly spasmed and lay a finger over Mia's mouth in instinctive admonishment. She then glanced about and, satisfied there was no one else in the area, heaved a sigh of relief.

"I know you meant well, but don't ever ask a question like that in the presence of an armsuit user or a mech driver! Those are two very opinionated and stubborn people groups, who have less in common than you might think," murmured Nikki with a dry cough. She then invited Mia to take a seat on *Silver*'s shoulder. "Let me see if I can explain it like this. You see that small mechanical suit over there, the one that looks like a sunken-headed gorilla?"

Nikki pointed down toward a machine, and Mia nodded when she saw it.

"That's a variant of the famous PAX 660. PAX means 'power actuated exoskeleton,' and it qualifies as the quintessential armsuit," said Nikki. "Rikeman owns that particular one, although he avoids getting in it anymore because he's so busy leading the rest of us. They can leap fifteen feet high from a still position and harness enough strength to crush bone between their fingers. I'm told the Altaire military has some slimmer models that are almost as strong and trade only small amounts of heft and resilience to allow them to be worn like suits of armor indoors. At the other end of the spectrum, some military forces design their armsuits with more bulk for raw strength or protection, but they tend to trade away their agility to do so. Suits like those strive to be like smaller versions of my mecha, although they'll never be a match for *Silver*, as I can smash those without even working at it. But heavy or light, if your real limbs stretch out inside the mechanical ones, then it's *technically* an armored suit, or 'armsuit' for short. In the hands of someone who understands how to use one, it's a devastating tool that can wipe out whole squads of infantry or harass unsupported vehicles into submission."

Nikki then leaned down and patted her mech beneath them. "Now, *Silver* here is a proper mecha. I pilot it from that cramped cabin you're sitting next to. Fully extended, my arms wouldn't even span the length of its shoulders, so it's obviously not a 'suit' so much as a machine I drive from inside with controls. Not all mechs enclose their pilots, but mine is big enough it can. They're slower and less wieldy than armsuits but strong enough to tip a tank on its side and use it as cover. It's a complex and short-range machine to put on a battlefield, but because they can muscle through such a wide range of tasks, their value is undeniable. The Rail Drivers generally have two to four present alongside the Paladin because of the sheer number of tasks they can be dispatched to perform. Are you following me so far?"

Mia felt embarrassed as she shook her head slightly and said, "I get that they're driven differently, but I'm a little confused. Why are you at a disadvantage against armsuits while piloting something as big and strong as *Silver*?"

"You really aren't familiar with modern warfare, are you?" said Nikki, her gaze softening somewhat as they sat idly on the mech.

"I'll try to spare you the history lesson and just explain the basic idea, but if you're smart, you'll look it up sometime," said Nikki. "To put it briefly, it's the same reason mechs almost never get any larger than fifteen feet tall. Sure, Singularity Dawn makes those thirty-foot monstrosities for intimidation, but they're not really practical battlefield assets because of the square-cube principle. Each time you double a machine's height, the mass increases eightfold, which is two *cubed*, but the same motor or rotor used to move it would only increase in strength by a multiplier of four, or two *squared*. For that reason, everything becomes progressively weaker, slower, and less responsive the larger you make it. My fastest movements in *Silver* still take five to eight times as long as anyone's reactions in an armsuit, and without them or infantry support, a couple of armsuit-wearing goons who know what they're doing could easily overwhelm me."

"Why do you use a mech and not an armsuit then?" asked Mia.

"It's the role. Think of a mech like a tank with arms and legs. Only an idiot would send a tank out alone, but with infantry support, it will mop the floor with its overwhelming firepower and ability to rip up fortifications and buildings." Nikki leaned in and added, "Besides, just because an enemy has the right tools to fight me doesn't mean they're automatically at an advantage."

"So it's a disadvantage, but only if all other factors like skill and expertise are equal," said Mia.

"Exactly!" said Nikki. "Don't get me wrong: A soldier in an armsuit can outmaneuver me, but not everyone who uses those things learns to utilize their gear to engage a mecha like mine. Most people think the big advantage of an armsuit is in the protection and strength, but it's actually the agility that makes them so frightening. The ability to leap around parkour-style like a squirrel, never slowing down for an instant, so your enemy can't get a beat on you. Not all armsuit users understand that, so while the technical advantage is there, infantry like you and mech pilots like me are not always as outgunned as you might think."

"What should I do if *I* encounter an armsuit?" said Mia.

Nikki sobered at this comment, as if she'd been reminded how new Mia was to all this.

"Well, offhand, I'd say don't engage it alone if you can help it," said Nikki, "but if you have to, just do the same sensible things you would against any soldier. They still have to take cover like you do, and they are still vulnerable in open fields and tight spaces. Just remember that an armsuit soldier can leap like a frog and bodycheck you from a standing position thirty feet away."

"Sounds like Tyber," said Mia.

"Sadly, Tyber won't be able to stop them for you. In all likelihood, an armsuit with a hold on Tyber will end very badly for him unless you're there to stop it," said Nikki. "Has he encountered such things before?"

"Not directly, but he's aware of what they are. Still, I should probably talk to him about it so he knows to be cautious," said Mia in reflection. She then smiled, wishing to pivot to a lighter topic. "So I noticed you and Eli both wear those spiffy black jackets. Were you two an item at one point?"

Nikki reddened at this comment and glanced away. "Th-The Raiden Alliance gives these to people who've helped them. Eli simply got that jacket for his time working with us." As she stared into the distance, she added, "There was a time he used to fight for our cause as well."

"What do you mean 'used to'?" Mia asked.

"Exactly what I said!" said Nikki angrily, then sighed. "Look, if you want the details, go ask him. It's not my business to explain someone else's loyalties. I trust him, and we've fought together. That's all there is to it."

With that Nikki slid down from her perch and invited Mia to walk back with her to the bunkroom.

CHAPTER 11

Treasure Hunt

Rikeman's briefing to the crew before landing was general but instructive, and Mia sat with quiet interest along with the others as he read it out to them.

"Zengin III is a desert wasteland consisting of two habitable polar regions separated by an equatorial hell, and home to a truly ungodly amount of wrecked infrastructure. The disagreement we're partaking in is between two corporations who have made competing claims to a set of wrecks and ore deposits, and we've been called in to help if the situation spins out of control. The group we are assisting is called Desert Rose. They are a sand-dredging and salvage company, and they're taking advantage of a dispute their competitors in the SanMontos trade cartel are currently having with the colony on the planet Medina. Since the cartel's resources have been tied up in a blockade aimed to bring the other colony into submission, Desert Rose has been making its own efforts to push back on behalf of the world by making aggressive grabs at the cartel's resource claims here on Zengin. However, Medina's people seem to be on their last leg, and with the rising possibility of SanMontos finishing its business and returning with its diverted combat resources, efforts are being made to reach a settlement early."

"Sounds kind of halfhearted for an attempt to put pressure on the terraforming cartel," muttered Nikki aloud. Mia found herself gently nodding in agreement.

"You aren't wrong, but it's not our place to tell our clients how to manage their affairs. In this industry, it's better to take your noble sentiments where you can get them. We're pretty picky who we work for, but as mercenaries, our clients won't always be saints," said the captain with a grunt. "Personally, I'm hoping the Global Union will finally get its act together and investigate the SanMontos blockade like it's supposed to, but then I've never put a lot of faith in those paper pushers. The odds of things going the colony's way aren't good, given we've heard virtually nothing from Medina itself lately. The important thing for us is to support the Desert Rose salvagers here on Zengin III. It's good money, and in terms of contracts, it's clean and low risk, as we're literally there to intimidate the opposition out of picking a fight."

Mia knew a little about Zengin III by reputation. Like many colonized worlds, it had at one point been a premiere world slated to become a paragon of terraforming and, according to many, had once held extremely promising projections. However, when its star expanded unexpectedly, the planet turned into an arid wasteland, forcing most of its inhabitants to the polar regions. This left many wealthy investors with most of their resources bleaching in what Rikeman had rightly termed the "equatorial hell" that formed about its equator, and much of the planet's history since had been filled with conflicts to salvage the vast resources colonists had been forced to abandon. Indeed, salvage was the high-risk venture no one could seem to give up on Zengin, for although the equatorial regions were ruled by firestorms and oppressive temperatures, the shifting dunes continued to reveal new deposits to tempt the investor who wanted to play treasure hunter. Whether it was raw materials, abandoned goods, or hardware left by a previous crew that had not fared so well, Zengin III drew scavenger crews like a magnet.

What agriculture did occur there required use of industrial greenhouse domes, as living near the polar "dust caps" meant the sun only rose and set once every orbit. For sociologists the two polar regions were a popular case study on cultural drift, having formed simultaneously by the same cataclysm, and from roughly the same array of people groups, yet separate enough that they'd developed quite independently of each other. It so happened that the Rail Drivers' client, Desert Rose, was a salvage group from the southern dust cap.

Upon landing, it became clear the operation was massive. Huge digging tools scooped, swept, or blew away sand to reveal ruined structures beneath, where more delicate methods were being implemented for excavation. In a sense it looked like a crazy archeological expedition, complete with geoscoping teams combing the surrounding dunes and workers carefully lifting ancient-looking items from their resting places. It also seemed hard to believe their small detachment could be a significant addition, as the salvagers seemed armed to the teeth and utilized immense rover-type vehicles.

"You gotta be kidding me! Is scrap really worth this much?" Mia asked Nikki as they began unloading their supplies.

"It's more than just scrap," said Nikki with a smile. "Terraforming machinery isn't simple stuff. It requires ridiculously efficient use of energy. It's some of the most sophisticated hardware we can build. True, lots of it is broken, but even wrecked, such machinery often contains a wealth of rare compounds. I remember reading about this place a few years ago. Lots of investors built high-end facilities and stockpiled materials before the sands blew in. The Global Union even wanted to stake a claim back when terraforming still looked promising. Add it all up, and you get heaps of fine goods and tightly regulated tech waiting to be claimed by the first one to find it. We may even take a large part of our cut as salvage goods, depending on what Desert Rose comes back with."

"Wouldn't those materials have been reclaimed immediately after the planet's atmosphere changed?" asked Mia.

"Well, knowing where to find it is one thing. It's getting there and digging it up that's the challenge," said Nikki as she began climbing into her mech. "Spacecraft can't just land out on site either. Not unless they're willing to truck their ship out with the scrap. Dust and sand are hard on machinery, and that goes double for anything that flies."

"I see," said Mia. "Back on *Megalodon*, we'd have salvage teams that would descend upon space wrecks the same way. At one point I even got handed a space suit and was asked to stuff everything that looked valuable into a ship's hold, despite having no spacewalking experience. It was good money, although in hindsight it's a miracle I didn't get myself killed."

Some way off, Rikeman could be heard arguing with one of the lead salvagers.

"No. Our contract was to man *your* guns and facilitate patrols. The only exception was the three mechs led by Nikki, and that was an independent contract you made with her. We are not bringing our biggest land vehicles along to haul your finds! Our job is to protect your perimeters and patrol for interlopers. If necessary, we can provide intel and reconnaissance," declared Rikeman.

"Then how do you expect to protect our excavator teams?" asked the salvager.

"On the backs of your LAVs and dune runners," said Rikeman. "They're the only vehicles that can withstand the conditions of the fire belt. I've compromised already by meeting you at your forward staging area and not further south at New McMurdo."

"The idea was to *prevent* our vehicles from getting targeted!" retorted the salvager.

"If you have extra vehicles for us to use, I'm sure we could buffer your sites more, but unless you plan on getting us tires for our APC, the Paladin stays in the *John Henry*."

"We're going to need a deposit on the vehicles you use then, and if it means your hardware will be on the line with ours, then I'll get your APC a set of camel shoes. Like I said, I need partners in this endeavor, not just grunts."

"Fair enough," replied Jack, "I'll get the ship's engineers out here to help with the refit, but we'll have to amend our contract if that's how you want it. Forger and Lambert can help you fit a set of desert wheels on the Paladin."

The sun was almost completely set, but it didn't take standing long in the remaining sliver of light to realize how oppressively powerful its rays were. Mia'd been told the rule was to stay covered up and avoid Zengin's sunlight, and had applied a generous amount of specialized sunscreen, but it was only too clear why they were going to operate almost exclusively by night. The sunlight's heat was merciless. Mia did her best to move her gear and watched Nikki as she evaluated her red mech, running tests to make sure the cooling systems were in peak condition for the same obvious reason. Nikki looked anxious as the beads of sweat rolled down past her face and onto the constricting jumpsuit.

"Is everything okay, Nikki?" asked Mia at one point.

"Fine," said Nikki. "*Silver* here just hasn't had to blast the cooling systems up this high in a while, so I want to make sure it's in prime shape."

Mia smiled and made no argument, for while Nikki's work interested her, she felt she needed to focus on her own mission preparation. She set about dressing Tyber and herself for the mission. True to his word, Eli had the gear he'd modified prepped and arranged neatly for Mia. Next to Eli stood a tall, muscular man with a hard gaze. He seemed expectant of her and waved for her to join them where Eli had the modified gear prepped and arranged.

"You two look ready for a fight," said Eli, noting Mia's outfit and Tyber's harness. "You might have already met this man, but let me introduce you anyway.

This is Sergeant 'Evski. He's going to be your lead and instructor for your first outing."

"Pleased to meet you sir," said Mia, reaching out a hand.

The man before Mia was an intimidating figure dressed in a range of military tans and greens. He had a scar along the bridge of his nose, with a second along his jawline that accented his steely gaze. He did not immediately accept Mia's hand and spoke with a heady voice mired in a thick accent as he replied to her.

"Our time is limited, but Captain says he has faith in your skills. I'm aware he also walked you through most of this mission and how to prepare for it. We go out with first wave to scout new excavation zone. He thinks you and tiger's skill will be of great use in recon and scouting, and I'm inclined to 'gree. But there is more to role than move getting about quickly and quietly to look. You will feel every ounce of equipment you have, so think hard as you pick."

From that point, the sergeant sat Mia down with an array of her gear, and pointed to each item, asking her thoughts on its role and whether she should bring it, discussing it at length. Mia appreciated the thorough approach, even if she felt it had an element of overkill, and tried to listen attentively.

"I was only able to get a few things modified, but I did manage to get these ready the way we discussed earlier," said Eli brightly as he pushed the submachine guns closer to her.

"Ignore technician's suggestion for weapons," said 'Evski nonchalantly as he pushed the tweaked weapons away again. "Lambert has too much faith in plasmatics and their piercing power. The last thing you need in recon is to have tracers giving exact position away every time you shoot."

Eli clearly didn't like this comment, but he made no attempt to contradict the sergeant. Taking her instructor's recommendations, Mia changed her selection accordingly. She did, however, insist on carrying the handgun Electra had given her. 'Evski didn't seem bothered by it and, after asking to look the gun over, said, "This is good weapon. Well used by last owner. How did you get it?"

"It was a gift from my mentor," said Mia.

"A close friend indeed, to part with something so personal. Its wear tells many stories," said the sergeant, returning the sidearm. 'Evski then pulled out a pair of canisters that Mia immediately recognized as hand grenades of some kind.

"Have you ever used smoke before?" asked 'Evski.

"No, but I'm a quick study," said Mia. "Are they dangerous?"

"Not in themselves, but they are a staple of our work. Just pull the pin and try not to 'throw like a girl,' as they say," said 'Evski with a wink and a grin. Mia smiled, deciding the comment was meant in good humor.

"We adjust the mixture with a special microchaff," said Eli. "It's an old Caladrian trick to foul up EM-based vision."

"Yes, it is another modification from our technician friend here. You throw when in danger and have no cover. Take care, though. Smoke, like tracer, works both ways," admonished the sergeant. "Is also no substitute for real cover. Don't think you're safe just because you're obscured. Our mission tonight is routine. We arrive as night sets in. Will be looking for promising salvage and, of course, possible troublemakers." He nodded as if Mia knew what he was talking about.

He continued, "I'm going to make it little more interesting, though. I'm headed out with advance party and will be on patrol when Pal arrives. I intend to hide partway through your route. You two will attempt to track me down without getting lost. If you want to impress, try get close without letting me seeing. If need, can reach by radio, but no chitchat. Since we're on desert world, I choose code names to theme. I answer to Sinbad, and we call *Pal*, our home base, the Roc, which will keep eagle eye on you with air drone. We call you Jasmine and striped friend Raja, like in children's story," said 'Evski with a chuckle.

"What children's story?" asked Mia.

'Evski paused to explain, then simply shook his head and said, "Never mind. Just board Pal when it's ready, and it will drop you off at appropriate starting point."

"The *Pal*?" asked Tyber, confused.

"I think that's a nickname for the Rail Drivers' armored personnel carrier, *Paladin*," said Mia, pointing to the name on the large six-wheeled transport they were near. "It's that vehicle the salvagers are asking us to bring along with them."

Tyber nodded. "So it's like when people call him Lambert?" he asked, pointing his nose at Eli.

"More like when I've called him Eli for short instead of Elias," said Mia, "or perhaps if I asked 'Evski to shorten my callsign to Jazz, but let's not get sidetracked. Sergeant, what should we do if we encounter someone else out there?"

"Most likely we only find scrap to tag, but in unlikely event you encounter something else on patrol, report sighting and return. We are scouts. We do not to engage if can be helped. Wear visor in case. I can link to it and see through if there is something you don't recognize."

"We won't let you down, sir," said Mia, hoping she sounded confident.

'Evski's expression remained stupendously unmoved, but he nodded in acknowledgment and said, "Then I see you out there soon."

With that, the sergeant jumped into the nearby LAV—a small rover not unlike an oversized dune buggy—with several other men before it took off across the sand dunes. Boarding the *Paladin* with Eli and Lynlee, they prepped to follow behind.

"Sorry your modifications didn't go over well," said Mia to Eli as they climbed the ramp.

"I expect 'Evski's just concerned that a good weapon will make you overconfident. I hate to admit it, but he's right that it's not a good primary weapon for this mission. But then, I think he forgets that as a beast trainer, your primary weapon isn't a gun at all," said Eli, glancing down at Tyber, who seemed to appreciate the remark.

"That's true," said Mia, running her hand through the tiger's hair fondly.

The *Paladin* was a surprisingly spacious vehicle, and Mia wondered why she was surprised when she saw Eli take his seat at the driver's wheel.

"Didn't you say you were a technician?" asked Mia.

"That doesn't mean I can't drive. I'm one of the few Rikeman trusts to drive this thing besides himself," said Eli with a grin, setting his seat into position. "I'll have you know, I'm also a decent pilot."

"You? Fly?" asked Mia dubiously. "Why is this the first time I've heard about it?"

"Who do you think is flying the drone that'll shadow you?" said Eli.

"Oh, you meant drones." said Mia, keying in on an opening to tease. "And here for a moment I thought you meant you flew real ships."

"I can fly those too!" retorted Eli. "Small ones, but ships nonetheless! Sheesh, you make it sound like I'm only good for fixing things!"

Mia chuckled at this remark and had to race back to her seat to avoid getting thrown about as the *Paladin* lurched forward. The large wheels made the dunes a smooth ride, albeit one with plenty of dips and rises that kept the trip entertaining. They had traveled for roughly two hours with the first deployment as the night set in. As the boarding ramp opened and Mia disembarked, she stopped short and gazed out into the night. The air was still mildly warm, and the stars beckoned from above the dunes ahead, backlit by the planet's rings.

"All right, Tyber, let's go find out where 'Evski is," said Mia.

With that, Tyber loped forward onto the sand, and the two proceeded into the night.

CHAPTER 12

Field Work

Tyber had an idea of what he was looking for, and Mia, a good grasp of the route they were supposed to take. It was a serene event, walking across the dunes. They weren't far from aid, but as they'd been instructed to refrain from idle chitchat over the radio, the silence made Mia almost feel like she and Tyber were wandering alone. She watched their surroundings with care, trying to take note of anything she could, but only the occasional small gust or shooting star disturbed the still landscape. Above, the silent drone piloted by Eli and Lynlee flew at a gentle lilt.

"I have something," said Tyber at length. "I think it's him, but it's muddled."

"Muddled? How so?" asked Mia.

"I think he is trying to mask his scent," said Tyber. "It goes in the right general direction, and there is so little else to smell that I don't think it could be anything else."

"Okay, but let's not let our guard down," said Mia.

They trekked across several dunes, and Tyber was diligent not to outpace Mia's stride, though occasionally

Mia would still ride on his back for short stints. Then, as they were walking, Tyber suddenly crouched down and lay still.

"What is it?" Mia asked in a whisper, taking her position beside him.

"The scent has changed. There is something nearby."

For a time, the two simply lay in wait as Tyber surveyed the landscape. Overhead, the drone could be seen circling gently just ahead of them. They'd agreed they wanted to catch 'Evski unawares if possible, and to this end, Mia was content to follow Tyber's lead. They had not stayed idle long when Mia turned to see a gun barrel pointed toward the same horizon they were facing. Donning her visor to confirm there was someone underneath, she saw a subdued heat signature buried inside the slope of sand and chuckled.

"Wow, I still have a lot to learn, don't I," muttered Mia quietly as she raised her visor, but the response that came made her blood run cold.

"Jazz, we're looking through your visor, and . . . that's not Sinbad," said Eli in hushed urgency. "Don't say a word, and stay very, very still. Given the position he's in, I think he's distracted by our drone. Lynlee is already running to get Jack. Are you getting this, Sinbad?"

A shot rang out in the distance as if in response, and Tyber watched in startled intensity but did not move at all from his place. A single streak of light crossed the night sky, piercing the drone where it flew, and all that followed in Mia's headset was static.

Mia's heart raced as she tried ever so slowly to inch her way up to Tyber's alert ears. She whispered as softly as she could, "Tyber. To your left. It's *not* 'Evski."

Tyber's ears twitched, and he held stock still, then suddenly lunged headlong into the sand, causing Mia to slip clean off her perch beside him. Tyber grabbed the figure from the sand. The man beneath flailed and tried to draw a knife, only to have the aggressing arm clenched in Tyber's teeth before he could clear the sheathe. Mia rolled and slid to a stop toward the bottom of the slope and lay sprawled in the sand. Standing, she looked behind her briefly. She'd landed on something hard that lay concealed just beneath the sand, but she felt she had little time to investigate it more as she scrambled back up the slope to cover Tyber with her handgun. The stranger stood stunned, his expression frozen in surprise.

"Nicely done, Tyber!" said Mia. "Hold him still for me. Now talk! Who shot down my air drone? How many of you are there?"

The man snarled, "Go to h— aagh!" his retort cut short as Tyber clamped down on his arm. Mia tried to ignore the cracking sound coming from the forearm as she pressed her interrogation.

"Bad answer," said Mia. "My friend doesn't like backtalk, so better make your next words count."

"You want my name, look at my tags, and if you want numbers, it's dozens!" said the man succinctly, trying to hide his trembling form as his arm pulsed with pain.

"He's lying," growled Tyber, trying not to loosen his grip on the man as he spoke. The man stared in wild panic at the tiger.

"D-Did it just talk? Ow! Fine, there are only four of us, but we have remote sand skimmers and mechs on standby only a call away that could gun you down in an instant!"

Mia reached down and plucked the radio from the man and held the receiver to her ear.

"Hey, give that back!" yelled the soldier.

"Shut up. Tyber, put a foot on his chest to keep him quiet for me. Remind him how heavy you are if he gets fussy."

Tyber complied, and the man maintained his silence nervously as Mia listened carefully to the signals coming in. There were at least two other men talking, one of whom was reporting the takedown of the drone, and the other in turn asked for a status report.

"Sounds like they're unaware of us," said Mia. "Now tell me which way the others are, and you might get to go home without any lifestyle-changing experiences."

The man seemed to wheeze out his response in what Mia could only describe as a pitiful attempt to raise his voice.

"Don't patronize me! I represent the SanMontos Cartel! Unless you call off your striped monstrosity, I'll have both your hides!"

"Duh," said Mia derisively, "of course you're with SanMontos! I figured that much out. Your gear shows you're not small-time, and SanMontos is the only other major player that's had eyes on this area. Looks like you don't have any breath left to speak, so unless you like passing out, I suggest you point them out."

The man was obstinate but pointed with his off arm toward the far dune, then toward the area Mia had seen the shot come from.

"And the third?" asked Mia.

"They're probably a pair to guard vehicles they came on," said a voice from behind Mia.

Mia whirled around to see Sergeant 'Evski crouching only feet behind them.

"This one is spotter for one that shot our drone," explained 'Evski without a pause. "When you stopped and the drone started circling, they thought they'd been discovered and choose to shoot. I thought about calling, but based on what I heard on radio, it seemed you had this well in hand, so I decided to play it safe and look for you myself. I did not expect whole group camped out like this. They must be guarding something."

"Don't think that you'll catch us all! They're probably coming to find me since they haven't heard me report in. They know you're here too, and now that we've shot down your drone," the man said, then paused to suck in short breaths as Tyber had not let up on his chest.

"Notice how he always follows admissions with threats," said Sergeant 'Evski. "He's either very bad liar, or he's baiting us. Still, does not change our next action. If you can guard him and make sure he not escape, I'll verify the whereabouts of others. Then we take this one back for questioning."

"If it's just two or three of them, we could take them," said Mia, "especially if that gunner who shot our drone is by himself like this one was."

'Evski smiled and said, "I like how you think, but don't get greedy. We've established location is important. Your new hostage may yet have more to share. You've done fine so far, but let's not push our luck. I confirm where others are, and once I'm sure they not aware of us, we leave."

Mia wanted to say more but decided to follow the veteran's lead. After 'Evski helped her securely tie up her hostage, he raced down the slope, up the far dune, and down the far side.

Mia watched as he crested the far dune and waited patiently. The silence now seemed oppressive, and the suspense, unbearable. She wanted something to do. Thinking back over the scuffle, she then remembered the curiously hard landing she'd had, and wondered if she'd encountered something she could tag for the salvage team later. Stepping gingerly down the sandy slope, she retraced her tumble and began sweeping away the sand. About two inches beneath, she began to find a solid surface. It was flat and smooth, and this piqued Mia's curiosity all the more. Could this have been what the men were protecting? After a little more digging and feeling about, Mia found the features of a wide, slightly slanted trap door with handles. It was hard to tell the exact dimensions, as the sand kept sliding over it so that digging it out was an all but futile process, so she decided to simply try the latch. Straining to lift it, she managed to heft it a few inches before Tyber tipped his nose under the gap and flung it open the rest of the way in a single stroke. Sand gently poured in from the slope above as they stared into the space below. It seemed empty and dark, and there appeared to be a steep set of stairs leading down.

"Wow. Talk about your secret passageways," said Mia as she looked into the space below.

Tyber sniffed cautiously and glanced between it and Mia before asking, "M'lady, shouldn't we tell the sergeant?"

"Probably better to show him," said Mia. "He should be back in a moment." As she glanced back at their prisoner, her eyes spotted a flickering light beyond the edge of the slope, causing them both to initiate a brisk return to the top of the dune again. They reached it to see several headlights moving toward them over the dunes. It seemed what the man had said about drones and mechs being available to reinforce them was true.

"Sergeant, er, Sinbad, sir, we have trouble," called Mia into her wrist link. "I see lots of bad company coming fast over the northwest dunes."

"Aagh! Leave it to me to lecture my student on getting greedy for intel, then making very same mistake," said 'Evski with a sneer over the comm line. "No doubt our prisoner's friends reported air drone, then called for help when he didn't check in! Get out of there! Run for it! With little luck, I'll be able meet you before you reach the—"

The line closed out in static, and gunfire erupted from the direction 'Evski had gone, indicating he had his hands full. Mia ran down the slope again, this time pulling the tied soldier along. She glanced at the open doorway and into the dark entrance, pondering whether or not it was a good place to hide. The sound of the vehicles was getting closer fast, and it was clear there would be no outrunning these pursuers if they were spotted.

"Tyber, get in," said Mia as she shoved the man into the entrance. Tyber glanced hesitantly at Mia but did as instructed, and she stepped down the stairs behind them, pulling the door shut. They stood motionless in the dark, and Mia kept her gun at the ready, though she wondered what she would actually do if anyone entered.

More gunshots sounded overhead a few seconds later, and several times, she heard vehicles pass near the entrance before whizzing off again in the frenzy of revs, whirls, and bullet impacts that followed. Small traces of sand steadily fell in through the edges of the door as they listened. Gradually, the sounds became more dispersed. Mia's eyes rapidly adjusted to the darkness, allowing her to take note of the chamber in short order. The room was unadorned, with only a single passage to the far corner from the short stairway she stood on. Not wanting their prisoner to give them away, Mia hauled him slowly toward the passage leading deeper in. The words Roof Access ran across the back of the open door, and beyond it she found another, larger stairwell leading down. As they stepped further inside the cavity, the man managed to cut his hands free on a bent edge of the door frame, then wrenched himself free before rolling away. He seemed to think he couldn't be seen while he tried to remove his gag.

"What do you think you're doing?" asked Mia.

The man moved faster than she anticipated, and took a swing at her but missed by a wide margin as she evaded. He lunged forward, swinging violently but blindly. Mia backed away cautiously until she came against a handrail, forcing her to block one of his strikes. The man took this as some kind of opportunity and grabbed at her, but to little result.

Mia caught his hand and threw him headlong over her back and over the rail in one swing.

He flailed as he tumbled helplessly down the shaft. A gut-sinking length of time passed before she heard the telltale "smash" of her prisoner striking bottom before all returned to eerie stillness.

Mia cursed under her breath at this development and said with a grumble, "Grr! Come on! I wasn't *trying* to kill him!"

"Still, hardly the worst outcome," said Tyber in a low voice as he glanced cautiously over the edge.

"Whatever this is, it goes down quite a ways," muttered Mia. "Let's be careful as we look around. The further we are from that entrance, the less likely we are to be found. I suppose we should also search for our . . . prisoner."

The two walked down the stairwell carefully, as the whole room seemed somewhat uneven. Mia was surprised to find she needed very little illumination to see as they moved down each floor with cautious fervor.

She tried several of the doors only to find them jammed. Some seemed accessible, although Mia felt hesitant to explore them too far for fear of disturbing the decrepit structure and causing a cave-in. Many of the rooms beyond were dismal but whole. More interestingly, they did not seem despoiled, as there were unopened cabinets and crates that sat undisturbed.

"I'm no expert, but it looks like nobody's come through here to sack it," said Mia. "I know the theory was this was a location few people had been in until recently, but I never expected anything like this!"

"It does seem quite vacant," commented Tyber. "No one's been here in some time."

The doors further down were much the same, although on the lower floors, some halls and doors bulged like they were threatening to burst from their placements, which made Mia feel cautious in her exploration. However, the stairwell itself seemed mostly clear, and Mia felt compelled to see how far down it went, if only until she found something that could pass as a floor plan of whatever they were in. They'd gone at least three floors down and into an extended stairwell with no observable doors along it before a notification on her display stopped her, indicating an imbalance in the air, and the presence of an asphyxiating gas buildup.

"Hold it, Tyber. This is as far as we go."

Tyber halted accordingly, then glanced up, awaiting an explanation.

"My wrist display. The opssistant is telling me there's a carbon dioxide buildup below us. We travel down much further, and we risk suffocating."

Tyber seemed to ponder the statement thoroughly, and Mia was reminded of how he looked when she first explained outer space to him. He glanced at her wrist display, then down the stairwell again, then back at Mia and asked, "Does it . . . have a scent?"

"No. It's essentially what we exhale, so it has no scent we can detect. However, because it's heavier than normal air, it can collect in low places. It looks as if some of it has settled down here, no doubt because there's no air circulating."

Tyber said nothing but gave a skeptical look.

"Don't look at me like that! I know what I'm talking about!" said Mia defensively. "Back on *Megalodon*, there'd be reports of something similar occurring every so often because of some disruption to the ship's air circulation or because the ship changed course in some weird way. It always resulted in a hazard zone in the ship. Command would have to cordon it off until they got it fixed. Only people with breathing gear could safely go into it. I guess this means we've explored as much as we can for now."

Tyber and Mia looked down again, trying to see the bottom, but with so little light, it was clear there was no telling what depth their secret shaft had.

"What do we do now?" asked Tyber.

Mia sighed, "Wait and see, I suppose."

CHAPTER 13

Before the Dawn

Lynlee fidgeted, bending down under the console and pretending to check the drone control equipment again as she listened to the argument unfolding. Sergeant 'Evski had returned a little over half an hour ago and given his report, and was confused when he heard Mia had not already returned.

"Explain what you mean by 'she's not here,'" asked 'Evski, clearly disgruntled. "When I circled back, she and d'tiger already left!"

"I mean she never checked in, and her signal vanished less than half an hour after those bandits shot down our air drone," explained Eli.

"Ridiculous. Th'equipment must have fault," said 'Evski with a slightly aggressive wave of his hand.

"I checked it twice, and Lynlee is giving it the once-over herself now. The drone may be down, but its transceiver was completely intact until the cartel mercs moved in," said Eli. "I might also add, we were able to track your signal long after hers vanished."

As if in response, Rikeman showed up and said, "Well, I've calmed the salvagers down for the moment. You're lucky we managed to warn them you were on that skimmer, 'Evski, or you might have gotten a hotter reception than you wanted. Any word from our rookie?"

"Not yet," said Eli.

"Hmm. She might have panicked and turned off her display," suggested the mercenary captain as his eyes searched pensively.

"Or she's aware now is wrong time to be found," replied 'Evski. "Little girl is inexperienced, not stupid, and her companion lives up to his predator reputation. She maybe decided to sneak her way back. It is one of their stronger skills."

"That's uncommon praise, coming from you," said Rikeman. "Does that mean they managed to sneak up on *you*?"

"No," said 'Evski, "but they did manage to catch our bandit spotter in his hiding place undetected. Not bad for her first day out."

"'Evski has a point about her attempting to sneak back. Remember what happened when we tried to ping the salvage tags?" said Eli.

"What are you getting at, Lambert?" asked Rikeman.

"These tags use our signal to bounce back their own unique identifier. Strictly speaking, they can't be 'turned off' because there's nothing to 'turn on.' Yet Lynlee and

I have been trying to ping Mia's tags since we lost radio contact. If we can't ping her salvage tags, then it's more likely they are hidden somewhere beyond our comms altogether."

"It's Dune City out there! There's nowhere *to* hide!" Jack blurted out. "Those salvage tags only work for our purposes because there's virtually nothing out there to block them!"

"But if she's still hiding out there somewhere, we should go look for them!" said Lynlee, sitting up.

"And how do you propose we start? Right now, we might as well be suggesting that sand gnomes appeared and whisked them away to their magical signal-blocking castle," said Jack, rubbing his forehead as he turned to 'Evski. "Sergeant, do you think they could have been captured?"

"It fits what we know," said 'Evski, "but like I told Lambert, there was no sign of her or tiger when I circled back on skimmer. It would have to be cleanest and fastest capture I've ever seen if they were."

"So either our enemy is so well entrenched they can capture and hide someone in minutes, or our rookie is remaining elusive from all of us in the open desert with a pocket full of tracking tags," said Jack as he looked among his crew members incredulously. "Suddenly, the sand gnomes sound pretty credible. Hell, unless we have more to go on, we can't make a move, and dawn breaks in the next hour! Keep monitoring for a signal, and tell me the moment you get anything!"

For half an hour after Rikeman left, little happened.

'Evski left and returned about ten minutes later, having exchanged the skimmer he'd stolen for one of the salvagers' dune runners.

"Why aren't we out searching for Mia?" grumbled Lynlee as she pouted her cheeks in frustration.

"You think 'Evski would be hanging around here with an idling LAV if he had even the slightest idea where to look?" asked Eli. "He's here because like the captain, he thinks us pinging Mia's signal is her best bet for getting found, so keep watching for anything new."

Night was waning quickly. 'Evski paced back and forth, irritating Lynlee as she and Eli continued monitoring. The *Paladin*'s comfortable familiarity did little to alleviate their anxieties as they waited. The approaching dawn was slowly blotting the stars out one by one with its light. The wind gusted as the sun prepared to make its entrance, and had just begun casting hot rays on the tallest dunes when a new signal broke the silence.

"Jazz to Sinbad. Raja and I are on our way back and urgently need a lift. Repeat . . ."

Lynlee jumped up in her seat and fumbled over 'Evski, who had all but pushed her aside as he looked for a way to send a reply. The signal was strong and unmistakably Mia's, and it had appeared in tandem with the ping of her tracking tags.

"Can she hear me? Jasmine, this is Sinbad! Relay position. We'll meet you there in the Roc after I tell Lambert. . . . Where is Lambert?"

Lynlee turned to look behind her and saw Eli running at full tilt down the entry ramp of the *Paladin*, making tracks toward the LAV. Following his train of thought, Lynlee grabbed a remote comms system and hefted it on before running to follow. She couldn't help but enjoy 'Evski's confused questions like "Where do you think you're going?" as he followed her down the ramp.

"Get with the program! We're rescuing Mia!" she yelled back as she ran after Eli.

Piling into the salvager's swift dune runner, the trip was only minutes, and Lynlee had little trouble navigating them toward Mia's signal as Eli drove. They found her in a wide stretch akin to a salt flat strewn with rubble both manmade and natural. She was on Tyber, and the two of them were jumping between the long shadows cast by the debris, trying to avoid the ground that had already begun to bake in the sunlight. Behind, the heat-distorted silhouettes of vehicles cresting the dunes beyond could be seen, and distant gunfire could be heard, along with the puffs of blasted dirt and sand among the debris. Mia and Tyber appeared to be moving to avoid gunfire and stay out of range, but it was clear the cartel combat assets were closing in rapidly, and mortars and other arcing weapons were being deployed to shoot over the dunes and past the haphazard cover in the flats.

The machine was large enough to hold several people comfortably, but it seemed tiny as it sped down the massive sandy slope. Lynlee could feel the shocks bottom out as they hit the flatland, bouncing clumsily as it sped toward the pair at top speed, meeting Mia and Tyber where they were. Eli parked it protectively between the pair and any potential fire, and Seargent 'Evski opened the door and yelled, "Get in!"

Mia leaped in ahead of Tyber, who'd barely made it in when Eli accelerated, preventing 'Evski from closing the doorway properly, pinning the passengers to the back as the vehicle turned to return the way they'd come.

"Hold on tight!" ordered 'Evski to Mia and Tyber. "We're not out of trouble yet!"

The statement was accurate, for the sound of more mortar shells exploded about them, rocking the machine as it started swerving evasively.

"Mia! Tyber! Where have you been!?" asked Lynlee excitedly, "We were all worried about you!"

"Long story. I think I found something," said Mia.

"Can you believe someone suggested we pick you up in the *Paladin*?" exclaimed Eli. Mia looked up in surprise as she realized who was at the wheel, and she couldn't help but smile at the broad grins reflecting back at her in a rearview mirror.

"That's true!" said Lynlee musingly. "I mean, it's got *some* speed, but we'd have taken ten extra minutes if we'd tried to pick you up with that! Tyber, try climbing up between the front seats so you won't tumble as much."

The small LAV bounced along the rocky flat before running up the sandy slope again like a skittering rodent, speeding straight for the top of the first dune.

"Buckle up and hold tight!" yelled Eli. "We're airborne in three, two, one!"

Lynlee held her hands up with excitement, and Mia clung to her chair as the vehicle caught air and landed on the far side.

"Best . . . rescue . . . ever!" yelled Lynlee. Tyber fought to remain on his feet and had begun using the front seats as a brace to hold himself between, but it was only partially effective, for he still ended up bashing his head against the console as the craft struck ground again. Tyber regained his footing in time to see out the narrow windshield. The glare made gauging the oncoming terrain difficult, and it felt like Eli was driving by feel as much as sight as they swerved around a rise.

Then, as they rounded the bend, they saw a salvager vehicle approaching from ahead, its guns firing past them furiously. Another followed. Lynlee looked behind them to see the enemy sand vehicles closing in with their superior speed but falling to the salvager's fire. Soon, there seemed to be a roar of engines and guns from every angle as both sides endeavored to circle their targets, then swerve to evade enemy fire and avert collisions.

"That's an awful lot of vehicles. Are there seriously Rail Drivers in all of them?" asked Mia in confusion.

"Some of them. Others belong to Desert Rose," said 'Evski with a chuckle. "Believe it or not, after I gave my report, Jack had hard time talking them down from assaulting site immediately. I can't tell if they are eager for shootout with cartel or just little overzealous at the thought of new dig site. One thing is sure: There is a lot of pent-up anger toward SanMontos!"

'Evski was right, for the fight was furious, taking place on every side. The Rail Drivers didn't seem to be leading the fight so much as managing it for the salvagers, who were doing most of the attacking.

"Rail Drivers, form up around the retreating rover and ensure it's safely escorted back to the salvage command vehicle," called out Captain Rikeman over the radio. "Sergeant 'Evski, I want your scouting party on the command deck immediately! Lambert, you're lucky Nikki was willing to guard the *Pal* when you left it unmanned. Get back aboard it as soon as you drop them off!"

The command vehicle was a behemoth crawler with treads taller than the LAVs, or even the *Paladin*, and booms that overshadowed everything around it. Designed to shelter the other vehicles beneath and carry their salvaged finds on top in cargo containers, it served as the heart of the salvager operation and kept its position at a safe distance from the skirmish. As Eli parked their tiny LAV just beneath the crawler, Mia saw several mechs taking defensive positions, alongside heavier machines sized more like the *Paladin*. Sergeant 'Evski wasted no time in getting Mia and Tyber aboard. Aware she had no obligation—or desire—to stay with Eli on the LAV as he made his way back to the *Paladin*, Lynlee decided to shadow Mia, Tyber, and Sergeant 'Evski as they boarded the behemoth vehicle. They were promptly led to a room in the midsection of the crawler, where the logistical and living facilities were tucked away. Entering a conference room or control center of sorts, Mia was immediately inundated with questions by its occupants.

"Your sergeant reported on the location and what happened before we lost touch with you. However, until dawn, we'd lost contact, which has us all wondering what happened," the lead salvager inquired feverishly.

"Don't take this wrong, but since you didn't bring him, I think we'd also like to know what you did with the prisoner. 'Evski said you had one in tow when things took an unexpected turn," stated Jack, overruling the salvager's question.

"Yeah, about that," said Mia with a look of chagrin. "I'm afraid I dropped him."

"Ah, understandable," said 'Evski, putting a reassuring hand on Mia's shoulder. "Carrying two on Tyber would be difficult to manage while running from—"

"No, I dropped him a little harder than that," reiterated Mia. She then proceeded to tell the story of what happened in the chamber after she'd spotted the cartel reinforcements en route. As she spoke about the chamber, the lead salvager's eyes grew wide with excitement, and he started asking for details about it, often turning to his compatriots as they mumbled and pointed to the table, which looked to be a tactical map of the area.

"Ouch," said Jack when she'd finished explaining what happened to the hostage.

"And you say you never reached the bottom because you hit a gas buildup in the shaft?" inquired the salvage leader with a fixed gaze.

"Yes, that's right," affirmed Mia, "although I tried to keep the light to a minimum, as I was concerned someone was going to follow us down, so I've no way of guessing how far I really was from the bottom. Whatever it was, it kept going down after I hit whatever it regarded as the ground floor, and we'd gone down at least other two flights before my display started flashing CO_2 warnings."

"That's . . . promising," inserted a salvager. "Settled gasses mean the area has not been disturbed in some time. It may be a completely new find they've been trying to conceal from us until they had the manpower to excavate it quickly. We all know prolonged digs are an invitation for the competition to muscle in on the profits."

"What happened after that?" asked Jack.

"Well, in short, we waited," said Mia. "Those goons had set up outside the doorway, and with them moving around outside, we opted to sit tight and hope 'Evski would be back. I got the feeling they didn't realize we'd found the entrance, and given how hard we had to push to get the door open when we did eventually leave, it's likely the sand had filled right in over us again. Still, I would have given a month's pay to know how to set a trap or two inside the entryway, as we were worried they were going to wait out the daylight in there with us. However, when they fled the site just before dawn, we decided to risk making a run for it."

"Hiding there was risky, but it sounds like you made the right call. Do you think you could find it again?" asked Rikeman after she'd finished.

"Are you kidding? Like I'd forget to tag a find that good!" said Mia, brightening.

"Let me guess, you put it inside the chamber?" said Jack, his arms folding as his face assumed a look of resignation.

"Well, yeah. It's not like I could just drop it in front of the door for them to find," said Mia. "Why?"

"Well, from what we can tell, the reason we couldn't find or reach out to you earlier is that the structure was blocking our signals," explained Lynlee sheepishly.

"Oh, come on!" said Mia with exasperation as she realized her oversight. "And here I was sure I hadn't missed a thing!"

"Relax, rookie. It's not as if you had reason to know," said Jack. "It just complicates matters slightly."

"To be honest, what the girl is describing is unprecedented," said the lead salvager. "We knew this zone was widely untouched, but to our knowledge, there are no records of a structure of this nature. The question is what it might be. A downed ship? A lost expedition? Some kind of building project not listed in the public record? Whatever it is, it's a prime opportunity, and we need to press our advantage and learn what they are hiding. Do you think your scout could lead us back there reliably?"

"Mia can speak for herself, but for my part, I can guide you to general location by dead reckoning. However, better we move quickly. The wind will only pick up from here. The longer we wait, the less recognizable it will be," said 'Evski.

Mia thought for a moment, then turned to Tyber and asked, "Ty, do you think you can find that chamber we were in by scent?"

"Most likely," said Tyber. "I left a deposit there."

"Seriously?" asked Mia, wrinkling her nose. "Please tell me you're talking about the body."

"Promising as the idea sounds, Mia, it's a moot point right now," injected Rikeman. "The sun is up, and it's already hotter than Africa outside. We'll discuss the next steps to take while you three take a break to unwind and rest up for your next assignment."

"Would I be out of line if I ask what happens now?" asked Mia.

Rikeman glanced at the salvagers, who looked at each other before one shrugged and said, "Nothing's certain. The most we can do for now is collect whatever scrap was left from our firefight with the cartel. It will take time to move our operation to the site of contact. Could we bother you to pay a visit to the command vehicle's navigation cab? Any insight you three can provide our drive crew would be invaluable."

"Sure. Which way do I go?" asked Mia.

"I can show you," offered Lynlee.

Lynlee led Mia enthusiastically to a small cabin that housed the driver of the crawler. Mia was glad to have the guide and found the vantage point exceptional as she peered through the tinted windows, for it was an enviable view of the surrounding desert. The helmsman seemed to know what she was there for, and he wasted no time asking her about which direction they were headed and what terrain she'd encountered, aiming to avoid any sharp rises and falls he could.

Once he'd established what would make the smoothest path for the land titan to inch its way there, the helmsman bid Mia and Lynlee good-bye and let them head to a cooler section of the ship. That was not to say the nook reserved for the Rail Driver crew members was exactly cool, but it was better ventilated, which made it much more welcoming than other parts. Mia was amiable, but the excitement of her escape was finally wearing off, causing the tension she'd been suppressing to set in. She and Tyber also seemed to be coming to terms with the sheer heat of Zengin, for despite the blasting cooling systems, the inside of the vehicle was still sweltering with little reprieve. After they reached their nook, Mia had asked Lynlee to help her obtain a drinking bowl for Tyber, as well as anything she could rig up to create more of a cross breeze within the space.

Lynlee went in search of a functional container. By the time she returned, Mia had changed out of her armor, set up a fan or two, and was now preoccupied quizzing Eli, who seemed dodgy about her subject matter.

"It's a straightforward question. How did you know—"

Mia was interrupted by Eli, who said, "I know what you're asking, and I'm telling you to ask me again sometime, perhaps when we're back on the *John Henry* . . . but not here. For now we have a mission to prep for, and once Lynlee and I are finished setting you up here, we have work to do with the salvage engineers. I promise I'm not trying to avoid the question. It's just a matter of time . . . and *place*."

"Fine. I'm too hot to argue," said Mia with a bitter tone of resignation.

"I get it. The water and air conditioning aboard serve to make things survivable more than comfortable. I'm told we're pushing this rig pretty hard by trying to get it to move by day. Try one of Val's drinks from the cooler," said Eli, offering a bottle with an Inner Spring brand on it. "Our chief medical assistant is no slouch about her research when we land out anywhere new, and she tries to keep us stocked accordingly. Naturally, her prescription here is lots of fluids. She tells me these kick your body's natural cooling functions up a notch while hydrating you."

"Thanks," said Mia obligingly. "I'm still finding it hard to believe it's significantly cooler in here than outside. Tyber's feeling it too. I can tell."

"He is?" asked Lynlee curiously as she petted the tiger, who was basking in front of a fan letting the breeze blow through his fur.

"Tyber's as tough as they come, but I know him too well. I don't think he will ever admit he's uncomfortable, but I can still tell when the heat is getting to him."

Tyber had no trouble overhearing the comment but made neither acknowledgement nor objection to it.

"Well, don't let it be said you're a careless trainer, Mia," said Valerie, who walked in at that moment to check the status of her cooler. "Well, it's gratifying to know the drinks are going at the rate I hoped they would. If the buzz I'm hearing is even remotely accurate, we have a big night ahead of us. Speaking of which"— she turned to Lynlee—"the command crawler's head of engineering asked you and Lambert to start moving 'temporary ducts,' I think he called them. Apparently, he wants to rig up a way to circulate air to the bottom of this mystery chamber when we get there."

Lynlee slumped and replied, "Figures. Right when I get the chance to really talk with Mia."

"Come on, Lynlee," said Eli. "Valerie's right. Mia and Tyber need their rest, and we have ventilation to roll out. Just be grateful this isn't a scenario where we need to do it with breather masks on."

"It's all right. We'll be here," said Mia, who lazily ran her fingers through Tyber's fur and made herself comfortable for a quick rest.

At several points, Lynlee would glimpse in at Mia as she lay in the hammock she'd set herself up in. Mia in turn watched (though not particularly diligently) as Lynlee and Eli went back and forth, rolling spools of clad cable and plastic fabric ducts. She was keeping an ear open in case extra hands were needed, aware that while a technician's work didn't in itself seem all that remarkable, it was often critical to an even half-comfortable environment.

When Lynlee finally ran out of things to do, she returned to find Mia quite asleep, and she grudgingly accepted she would have to wait to ask Mia about her adventure until later. After making herself comfortable, she prepped her own tools and toys in anticipation of the mystery chamber. Admittedly, her role driving the hover drone to guide them was nothing major, but she took her role seriously as a remote assistant, and after practicing with its controls and reviewing its interactive manual for good measure, she waited anxiously. People quietly came in and out, spreading out in their borrowed corner of the giant crawler, usually to obtain a few winks of sleep in the noise and heat, but otherwise the area remained very dull, and eventually, Lynlee herself also dozed off until she was awakened by Valerie.

"Hey, doc. What's up?" asked Lynlee sleepily.

"I hate to do this, but do you know where Mia went?" asked Valerie. "I came in to find her, but she wasn't here."

Lynlee looked up at the hammock, which was now empty, and said drowsily, "I guess she stepped out."

"You weren't keeping her up with chitchat, were you?" asked Valerie with a hint of teasing admonishment.

"No! I mean, I wanted to, but when I got here, she—" Lynlee was cut short as a blood-curdling scream erupted from the washroom, causing her to jump to her feet beside Tyber and Valerie, and they all three started for the hall to see what was the matter. Before they could move very far, however, Mia stepped out, shaking her head and trembling in a mix of shock and self-deprecating frustration. After a second, she looked up at them in the dusk light of the dimming sunset now flowing into the chamber. Her eyes had an amber glow from the reflected light, and pointing to them with her fingers, she stammered, "T-Tapetum lucidum. That's what you meant. The reflectors in a cat's eyes, right?"

Valerie smiled and, stifling a laugh, replied, "Yes, Mia. They augment low light vision but sometimes come at the cost of overall clarity. Yours, however, seem particularly well polished, as you still have fairly sharp vision."

Tyber stared, as if debating whether to simply dismiss the whole reaction out of hand and go back to his dozing. This had a surprisingly calming effect on Mia, who gave a troubled laugh and said, "That explains a few things. Well, I'm awake now!"

"Aren't we all," said Valerie.

"I don't know. Your eyes look kind of cool in this light," said Lynlee with a smirk.

"So what had you up and about?" asked Valerie.

"Bad dream," said Mia in a subdued, but exasperated tone. "I knew I was working through some baggage, but hell if I could have expected it to catch me *now* of all times!"

"I've never actually known a time that was convenient, but I grasp the problem. Would you like to talk about it?" asked Valerie.

"Ask me again sometime. Aagh! Now I'm starting to sound like Eli!" said Mia. She reeled, then stopped and, as if shoving her feelings away from her, thrust her arms forward. "Work comes first. If there's one thing I learned while I was training, it's never fail to follow through. Work is no exception."

"That's right!" cheered Lynlee. "After all, we've got a tomb to raid!"

"Tomb?" said Valerie with a skeptical chortle. "What makes you think it's a *tomb*?"

Lynlee blushed, fumbling for a reply, when Mia came to her aid, saying, "Well, I did leave a body there, so technically . . ."

"Exactly! It's like a dungeon from a fantasy! There may even be traps and hidden treasure, for all we know! Once we go in, we—"

"You mean, *she* goes. *You're* staying here," interrupted Valerie.

"Am not!" objected Lynlee. "Lambert said I'm flying the hover drone and can help feed the temporary ventilation in from the command crawler."

"Fine. Fine. Just stay close to him. You and he are tech support, not riflemen. Speaking of which, Sergeant 'Evski says he wants to meet with you at the entry ramp you came in from. He's pretty sure we've zeroed in on the valley you found it in, but we're still combing the area for the chamber itself."

"Sounds like I'd better get a move on then," said Mia. "Let's gear up, Tyber."

CHAPTER 14

"Tomb" Delving

The crawler moved at little more than a walking pace, making for an easy dismount. Once they were down, the trek was little more than a hop and a step or two to meet Captain Rikeman and Sergeant 'Evski.

"Ah, you are here. Let's hope there is still something for Tyber to track that hasn't been incinerated by sun or displaced by wind," commented 'Evski.

"You sound like they have nothing to go on. Five reál says they find the entrance in under fifteen minutes," said Rikeman.

"I don't bet cash where I am not knowing. I merely stressing this could take long time," murmured 'Evski.

Despite 'Evski's concerns, Tyber had little trouble finding the entrance again, and before the crawler could even position itself over it, a protective tent had been erected around the door with temporary lights and power. In one corner, Eli and Lynlee fidgeted with gear Mia didn't even begin to recognize.

Once the door was clear, they cautiously opened the entrance again for exploration, and Mia began leading the crew down. With temporary lighting to hang behind them, the signs of her last visit were hard to miss. They showed footprints on the dusty floors and grates, and even divulged where the cartel soldier had gone over the rail. Eli stepped in behind them and began screwing a clamp to the railing as they looked down.

"Hard to believe this was all just under the surface," said Rikeman. "By the looks of it, we just crawled through the roof access of a multistory building."

"I thought you were exaggerating about this place," commented 'Evski, "but now that I've seen it for myself, I understand why you wished you'd learned lay traps. It is a labyrinth!"

Mia nodded in agreement, but before she began to descend, she turned to Tyber and said, "I'm afraid I need you to wait here this time."

Tyber did not reply. He simply circled in front of her obstinately. Mia gently stroked his head and replied, "Look, as much as I'd like to have you along, I'm not going to lose my partner to an accumulation of stale air. Besides, you'd be impossible to move if you collapsed suddenly."

"How will you fare any better?" asked the tiger.

"We're going down with breathing masks," explained Mia. "If we had one that could fit you, it'd be one thing, but . . ."

Rikeman piped up as she trailed off, saying, "It's actually been a problem the med tech and I have been discussing. We can't exactly buy Tyber breathing gear off the shelf, and Valerie only has a vague idea of his body's demands for air. For now, though, you need to stay here with Lynlee and Lambert. Once they've set up the vents to clear things out, you'll be free to join."

Tyber said nothing but seemed to acknowledge Mia's request, and watched dutifully from the top of the stairwell as they descended down.

"You know, Tim may actually have some insights on how to fit Tyber," said Rikeman. "He may actually know a way to design him a breather kit too. Even if he can't, he almost certainly knows someone who does."

"Breather kit? You mean like a face mask?" asked Mia.

"Or a helmet. Heck, give that man enough time, he may even make something spaceworthy for him. I'll prompt Valerie to send a bioscan of Tyber to him. Then you can ask him about it when we send you back to get your space suit."

Salvagers dispersed at every entrance and intersection, feverishly evaluating doors and deciding their next steps between reinforcing the chamber, clearing sand and debris, and traveling further in.

"No shortcuts when checking these doors!" Mia heard one of the salvagers yell as they went. "One wrong move and we'll drop enough sand to bury the lot of us!"

The workers carefully and methodically set about bracing and reinforcing the bulging doors and checking for signs of stress before attempting to open them.

"How much farther to the point you stopped at Mia?" asked 'Evski.

"Not far. Just look for where the tiger tracks stop," said Mia, glancing up at the temporary ductwork to be installed as it made its slow descent. It dangled behind them from the railings above like the malproportioned trunk of an oversized elephant.

When they reached the threshold, Mia found herself sputtering in surprise, as she wondered why her wrist display was not giving any CO_2 warnings as it had before, for she was certain she'd reached the dangerous point.

"Don't get too excited. Our movements are probably creating some circulation already," said Rikeman. "Even a little air movement goes a long way toward dispersing CO_2 buildup. That said, this still makes a good place to mask up."

The three masked up accordingly and, after running mutual checks, continued their descent. The contrast of their lights against the darkening ambiance made Mia feel like her vision was narrowing, and she was beginning to realize just how well she'd been able to see in the dark when she'd been there before.

"Now that I can glimpse the bottom, I see no fewer than seven flights. Two look to have originally been aboveground before the sand, and the other five go further below. Whatever this was, it was tall as well as deep. Perhaps our friends had plans to use this as a refuge or staging point," commented Rikeman.

While there was no CO_2 buildup to be found, there was a buildup of silt that had made its way down, and it marked the end of the stairs, signaling a "bottom" had been reached. Mia was relieved to find this silt buildup had also minimized the mess made by the cartel soldier, and 'Evski seemed to have come prepared, for he wasted no time in producing a tarp to cover the remains.

"I knew I'd be using lethal force sooner or later, but there's a dark irony that my first takedown would be someone I needed to make sure *didn't* die," said Mia disgruntledly.

"I think little girl is handling it pretty well, don't you, Captain?" said Sergeant 'Evski.

"Ah, figures there'd be a lock here too," said Rikeman, evading the question and turning to the drone. "Lynlee, I need Lambert down here with his tools."

"He's on his way. He says to dig out the entrance so we don't waste time getting it clear," was the reply from the drone's speaker. Not long after, Eli's quiet footsteps could be heard, and he wasted no time in evaluating the lock.

"Whenever you're ready," said 'Evski impatiently as Eli looked the mechanism over.

"I'm a technician, not a cipher. I can't just punch a code in for this thing, and even if I could, I don't think it'd open without outside help," said Eli as he began drilling. A moment later he'd threaded leads into the door, and the magnetic lock unsealed.

"Just prop this open and we're good. There's no power, or we would have had a major alarm, based on what I can see of this design," said Eli.

The door slid open and the group entered. Within was a long corridor that branched several times, but nobody felt the need to split up, and each selected the most straightforward route they could find. A handful of these branches led to small rooms resembling offices, barracks, or storerooms, until the main hall led into a large room. At first, the lights didn't seem to reach far enough to illuminate the far side. Then, as they advanced a short way in, the dim dimensions of the space came into view.

"Eagle mod!" exclaimed Mia, and Lynlee could be heard squealing with delight through the drone.

"Well, that's different," said Rikeman with a low whistle. Before them was what looked to be an abandoned missile silo, complete with a rocket in waiting. Beyond, the signs of a control room could be seen as well as a spiraling escalator that encircled the machine and, most disturbingly, a connecting rail system.

"Was Zengin III originally planning for a war?" asked Mia.

"I don't think this was theirs," said Rikeman, walking a short way around. "There's a Global Union insignia on this missile. Maybe the GU planned to make a head-quarters here, back when the expectation was this world would become a second Earth from which they'd play 'interstellar peacekeeper.' Building it while still in the terraforming process would make it difficult for anyone to monitor its creation. Sergeant 'Evski, climb up the silo stairs as far as you dare and let me know the state of the silo's hatch. I want to know if there's a risk of a cave-in. Lambert, take Mia and look for a generator. See if it's intact and you can get some power going. I'm going to check the control room ahead and see if there's a map for this place."

"Yes, sir," said Mia, following Eli and the drone.

"Well, let's have a look near those train tracks," said Eli, pointing his flashlight. "I expect the rail system draws from the same junction box we want to hook into."

The short stairway to the tracks felt unsteady but serviceable, and Lynlee's remote drone maneuvered slightly ahead into the tunnel to shed some light, churning the particulates that clung to the air as it went. Eli's eyes followed the cables that ran parallel to the tracks, searching for a point of divergence. The tunnel opened into a partially buried room filled with vehicles of varying sorts.

"Lynlee, have you shown this to the salvagers?" asked Eli.

"Don't have to," said Lynlee. "I have a crowd forming around me that's starting to block the entrance to the bunker. We—"

The comms cut out, and for a moment the drone stopped, hovering midair. Mia looked up, wondering what had happened. After a moment, Lynlee spoke again.

"Sorry about that. It looks like there's a commotion going on outside. I don't know what's up, but it's got the scaven . . . er . . . salvagers excited. They're asking for Jack to come back to the surface."

"Are you kidding me?" sneered Rikeman over the comms. "What the hell could they want me up there for? Aagh! Sit tight, crew. Tell them I'm on my way."

Mia gave a small sigh and resumed watching Eli as they walked toward the back of the underground garage, when a new sound caught her attention. It had been a quiet tapping that made no sense at first. Mia looked into the dark, then realized what she was seeing and nudged Eli, pointing.

Eli turned and looked in time to see a dim light from the far end of the tunnel to the one they'd entered by. At first, the contrast had been clear only to Mia, but just as a figure emerged with a dim light, Eli realized what she was perceiving. He turned off his light and snatched the drone out of the air, promptly deactivating it. Mia followed Eli's lead and guessed Lynlee was probably fuming at her console that he'd turned off the drone, but that could not be helped. One by one, they saw a set of four soldiers appear, armed and spreading into the facility.

The two of them quietly took cover as the men in the armsuits advanced. They looked to be headed to each major section.

Eli breathed his words, like the use of his voice would betray their position. "Looks like an advanced force. Some kind of power-suited commando squad. Not good, as this is definitely their environment to work in. Still, this isn't beyond us. Mia, you have cover and darkness, as well as your optic camouflage. If you can flank them and hit the one approaching us from behind, we have a shot at stopping them," said Eli. "I'll try to relay a message to Rikeman and 'Evski."

Mia's heart raced, but Eli had a point. Even without Tyber, she was a combat asset, and she had the gear 'Evski had prescribed for their last mission on hand. As Eli quietly relayed what was unfolding to Rikeman, Mia stepped out of the control room and moved as quickly and quietly as she could while keeping her head down. The soldiers had separated, and one was angling toward her, but he did not yet seem aware of her. She gripped her carbine carefully, and as the commando passed, she peaked behind and then turned to fire. To her dismay, while the shots connected, they did not penetrate, impacting and deflecting almost harmlessly off the armored plates and synthetic muscle fiber of the armsuit. The enemy commando turned instantly and leaped aside in a twelve-foot dive like a bolt of lightning, firing blindly in her direction before he vanished behind cover. For a second, Mia had lost sight of him and backed up hesitantly before firing again. This proved a mistake, for the soldier spotted her position and returned with directed fire as he leaped again before Mia could get her sights on him. He made a wall leap before landing ahead and advanced slowly, his gun trained on Mia's point of cover.

Mia was pinned in. She felt out of tricks and thought better of firing again, as she did not feel confident she could peek out of her corner in time to shoot at him, much less hurt him with that armor on. Yet as the armored commando stepped forward, a single shot sounded, and a streak of gold, violet, and azure flew from a trajectory to Mia's right, burrowing into the soldier's chest, leaving a hole that peeled back the plating and left a ring of carbon scoring around the entry. The suit that seemed so hard to damage before faltered, and the man collapsed in a heap. Mia glanced to her right to see Eli holding his modified handgun.

"Overconfident in their protection. Not so surprising," said Eli. "Still, this is bad. We came equipped for fights in the open desert, not enclosed spaces like this. Armsuits and powered armor like this have a mobility advantage in here."

"What did you shoot him with?" muttered Mia, glancing between his handgun and her carbine.

"My handgun. It's the plasmatic I showed you earlier. You know, like the SMGs I modified for you. Well, except yours are automatic and have perhaps a twinge less output, to optimize range. A handgun like mine isn't accurate at a long enough range to justify a lower output. The ones I modified for you will be able to fire two or three magazines before you drain the H-cells and—"

"Tell me the stats later," interrupted Mia. "Why are you packing one when I'm not?" Mia was reflective as much as inquisitive. "So that's what a plasmatic is capable of! I should have listened closer when you first explained it. I'm beginning to regret that I didn't listen to you over 'Evski. I sure wish I had those guns now!"

"Don't. 'Evski was only trying to look out for you. I would have argued with him if I'd thought you'd be up against armsuits . . . although if you don't rib him about it later, let me know so I can," said Eli with a chuckle as he began searching the corpse. "In a lot of other situations, a plasmatic's bright flash would have worked against you. However, getting his attention was your goal this time, so you could give me a clean shot, so it worked out."

"R-Right," Mia muttered, as she glanced away, content to let Eli believe her panicky second burst of fire had been deliberate.

"You don't think the others could have made it to the shaft, do you?" asked Mia, thinking aloud.

"Possibly, but they'll regret it if they do," said Eli. "Remember, Lynlee still has Rikeman, Tyber, and several others with her. Still, we'd better let the team know what's going on. Stay alert. I lost sight of the other three, and while I think they headed toward 'Evski and Rikeman, there's always the possibility one of them doubled back if they heard our firefight."

Eli fiddled with his comms, and eventually a tenuous signal came through.

"Lambert, do you copy?" they heard Rikeman asking.

"Lambert here," said Eli.

"Finally. They tried blocking our comms, but fortunately we had enough in place to compensate. Looks like they're approaching us with heavy firepower above, and we just had a run-in with two of their commandos on the stairwell. Poor Tyber tried pouncing one and nearly got thrown into a wall before I took care of him. I think he was taken back by the armsuit's strength. He looks a little shaken but uninjured. When the other guy realized we had firepower enough to grief 'em, he doubled back. He's likely in there with you and aware you're there. Sergeant 'Evski, what's your assessment of the missile hatch?"

"Missile hatch is seriously cracked," reported the sergeant over the comms. "Looks like weight of sand has damaged it."

"I'm counting on it," said Rikeman. "Eli, Mia, reactivate Lynlee's drone and get to the control room. If this missile silo is built like I think it is, then it should use explosive actuation to uncap itself. Pop it open, and we might be able to get Nikki down there in her mech to support you."

"Jack, I'm not sure that's a good idea," said Mia, remembering Nikki's words about being at a disadvantage against an armsuit. "Don't those guys move wicked fast in those armsuits? I'm not sure even Nikki would be able to hit them."

"You're not wrong. An armsuit's forte is in the mobility it gives its wearer over normal infantry, which is the perfect counter to a larger mech in solo combat, but it's not as bad as you think," said Rikeman. "I want Nikki down there to watch the railway tunnels, which are long and narrow. Once there, range and armor will become the key advantage. That and I think Nikki's good enough to get this guy. None of these goons are really utilizing their armsuits to their fullest, and it's not the first time Nikki's had to deal with stormtroopers like them. However, we need to move fast and secure that tunnel before SanMontos has time to send reinforce—"

A blast came from the direction they'd entered, suggesting the last commando had collapsed the way they'd come. Mia looked at Eli, who was busy reactivating the hover drone. The drone paused suspensefully for a second before cutting in with Rikeman's voice. "Did you get all that, you two?"

"Enough of it," said Eli. "I take it the plan hasn't changed even though he collapsed our way in?"

"For now. Lynlee, do whatever it takes to keep that armsuit off them. Call him dirty names and speak ill of his mother if you have to. Be as disruptive as possible."

"Got it, chief," said Lynlee.

"Lead on," said Eli to Mia.

"Me?" asked Mia in surprise.

"You're the one who can still see. If Lynlee's drone is the only one using lights, it's a pretty good misdirection, don't you think?" said Eli.

"Ooh tricky!" said Lynlee through the drone as she turned it in a new direction and took off. "I'd better go look for him then. Good luck, you two!"

"And you, Lynlee," said Mia as she took Eli's hand and started up a stairway. However, they made it only a few steps before gunfire erupted from the far end of the chamber, forcing Mia and Eli to duck for cover. Further fire was directed at the drone as they took refuge behind their corner, and Mia was quick with a smoke grenade, hoping it would do what the darkness wasn't, but as it burst and they began to run, Mia saw to her dismay the soldier had responded only by vaulting above the smoke and onto the stairs ahead of them in a stupendous leap. Eli was quick to fire his handgun, but the man dodged away again to a well-covered vantage, leaving them to awkwardly step around where Eli's shots had torn into the catwalk stairs. That was when Lynlee pulled through, for she'd simply rammed the soldier with the drone, causing no physical harm but thoroughly distracting (and irritating) the armsuit soldier, so that Mia and Eli managed to make it to the control room without being fired upon.

A blast of sparks and Lynlee's resigned "well, that's that" signaled her drone was down. Wasting no time, Eli grabbed the nearest brace he could find to bar the steel door (in this case, his pipe wrench) and, holding it in place, called to Mia, "Check the upper left panel. Start reading buttons for the hatch."

"What's it going to say?" asked Mia as she began searching desperately.

"Something like Silo Open or Hatch Off," said Eli as the soldier tried the door. The commando suit's strength came to bear, bending Eli's steel pipe-wrench and causing Eli to recoil his hand to avoid having it crushed.

"What good will pressing it do if there's no power to the hatch to open it?" asked Mia as she began pressing, almost at random.

"Explosive actuation," said Eli, "It's a standard practice for missile silos like these. They have to be able to open even in the event of a nuclear blast or an EMP, so they're designed to work without power."

Pressing several promisingly marked buttons, Mia looked up to seek assurance she was doing what she was supposed to, but Eli was thoroughly distracted as he tried anything he could think of to stymie the cartel soldier's attempts to break in. She was semi-gratified to hear something shudder above them in response to one of the buttons she'd pressed, and looked up to see what was happening, but sadly the silo cover remained in place.

Eli backed from the door toward Mia as the wrench and the door began to further deform under the strength of the soldier's armsuit. He asked in confusion, "Was that it?"

Mia opened her mouth to respond when a second, larger explosion shook the facility and fractured the silo cap, causing the same to cave, pouring seemingly endless amounts of sand in behind it.

"Oh gosh, I've killed us all!" thought Mia for a split second.

CHAPTER 15

Silver in the Sand Pit

Aboveground, in her red mech, Nikki leaped up at the first cartel mech she saw as it crested the steep dune, thrusting its torso upward. The attacking mech had traded its arms for heavier firepower at the shoulders for the desert battlefield, and Rikeman had correctly deduced they were planning to use these for long-range bombardment while their smaller skimmers ran interference ahead of them.

As a mech pilot, Nikki was acutely aware the principal advantage of bipedal mechs was their ability to grip, manipulate, and interact with their surroundings. The cartel mechs, however, had shortsightedly removed this trademark advantage for added artillery. Nikki smiled as she saw their heavy armaments. Lying in wait for the cartel mechs had paid off nicely, and at this close range, they'd have trouble aiming them at her.

As its allies turned to target Nikki and gain a firing angle, Nikki thrust her choice weapon into the robotic thigh gap formed by the legs and fired into the vulnerable walking assembly. The gun in question was the weapon the Rail Drivers were named for: the hypermagnetic rail mass driver, sometimes shortened to names like HRMD, mass driver, or rail driver. Its power was great but had a prohibitive recoil to infantry, so it seldom saw use except by heavy-weapon specialists or armsuit users. On a mech, however, it was a staple for penetrating most forms of armor. As the legs gave way, Nikki gripped the mechanical carcass as a shield and charged the next closest mech. The pale dim glow of the planet's rings in the waning light of dusk contrasted the flickering warm hues of cannon fire, illuminating *Silver*'s red paint in a curious spectrum of lights. The mechs fired on her position but could make no serious attack at her while their allies lay in a heap, forming Nikki's newly improvised cover. Reaching the next mech, which held a mortar assembly on its shoulders, Nikki engaged by swinging her last victim's leg under the mech and used it to force her new prey to one knee, high-centering it with the entangled limbs and giving her almost a standing level of cover, then proceeded to use her position to fire her mass driver at the remaining mechs. She still had multiple hostiles in a crossfire formation, but it was still more tenable than an open fight, and with her fellow mech pilots and the allied dune-runner teams now moving to harass the enemy's left flank, the risk she would become surrounded was waning.

"Nikki, come in!" called Rikeman. "The crawler reports you're not far from a missile silo we found. We've opened it up for you to drop down through."

"You mean that sinkhole that just formed behind me?" asked Nikki.

"That's the one. 'Evski, Lambert, and Mia are pinned in down there. Once you've ensured they're all right, move to cover the underground tunnel nearby so they can't bring reinforcements to hit us from underneath. Do you think you can plug the gap behind you once you're in?"

"I'll give it a try," said Nikki.

Pulling the mechs she'd piled up, Nikki hauled her pile toward the hole haphazardly while trying not to expose her frame to attack. As she neared the opening, she began to feel her ballast shift toward her, pushing her in as she slid down and dropped through the new opening. Behind her, the cartel mechs collectively fell, lodging themselves in the entrance behind her. She dropped onto the missile, which she clasped at the nose with one arm as she took point. Her mech's bright searchlights lit up the facility like daylight, and upon realizing he was outgunned, the armsuit soldier ceased his attempt to break down the door and made a dash for the tunnel he'd arrived through, endeavoring to evade with all the agility his exobionic suit had to offer.

"Yeah, you better run!" Nikki said as she fired at him from her high vantage. After verifying the area was secure, she checked for a way to drop to solid ground and called out, "All clear, you two. You can come out now."

"That's fine, but I'm afraid that goon bent the door out of shape! We can't get it open now," yelled Eli from inside.

Nikki shuffled toward the jammed door, taking measures to watch the cartel tunnel.

"Okay. Back away, you two. You never know when a crushed nut or split washer is going to decide it wants to become shrapnel," Nikki warned, then carefully pressed the door inward until the hinges broke.

"I can't believe that worked," said Mia with a tone of exhilaration as they stepped out. "I thought for sure that missile hatch had fizzled out on us or something!"

"That's because it did," said a familiar voice from far off. Mia looked to see 'Evski climbing over the safety rail and back onto the now bent and crooked catwalk, which appeared to have torn away from several of its placements near the hatch. The unsupported metal walkway swayed under him as he waved. "But not to worry. Nothing little C-4 couldn't fix."

"Don't tell me you seriously set that off while still on that catwalk!" said Eli in horror. "By the looks of things it nearly took the whole assembly out with it!"

"It was a risk, but time was short, so I split difference on safety and hung from far side behind sturdy metal sheet," said 'Evski, knocking on the bent panel lashed to the safety railing.

"That's an aluminium sign, you dingus!" yelled Nikki from within her mech. "What's more, if I'd chosen to catch the inspection walkway instead of the missile nose, it probably would have torn away completely and taken you on an eighty-foot ride straight down!"

"Relax," said the sergeant with a shrug. "I know you too well. You're too fond of *Silver* to risk breaking fall on flimsy walkway like this. Now, come with me so we can secure this tunnel. All of you."

"Are you sure you got everyone?" asked Nikki. "*Silver* is easily flanked by armsuits."

"I counted four," said Mia. "Eli got one for me, Rikeman says he dealt with a second, Nikki just drove off the third . . ."

"And I dispatched last one," said 'Evski, twirling a knife.

Mia felt a wave of both relief and unease as she asked, "Wait, you took down one of those 'so strong I could outhug a gorilla' armsuit commandos *with a knife*?"

'Evski shrugged and replied, "I got lucky. If the man had been Rikeman, it might have gone differently. However, poor chap thought he could strangle me bare-handed with all those synthetic muscles. He didn't realize I'm quick with knife and know where to poke. He's interred in sand now."

CHAPTER 16

In Other News

"And today, Governor Lorenzo of Medina voiced his thanks to President Kurtis Ghuli of the Global Union for his surprise appearance at the summit meeting between Medina and the SanMontos terraforming cartel to oversee the negotiations."

Mia tapped the screen to raise the volume as the news feed continued.

"The president's visit was prompted by concern for the colony's welfare after a report from undisclosed sources alerted him to the plight of Medina. The colony alleges that the terraforming cartel has been pressuring the colonial administration. The president declined to comment on how he obtained this information, although speculation circulates that his inside information might have been related to an entanglement transceiver that mysteriously vanished from Providence Starport on Caladria, believed to have been purloined by Caladrian confederates. Now, with the quantum entanglement network restored on Medina, new information is coming to light that the protective fleet surrounding the gateway may have served as an economic blockade. However, SanMontos assures the public that its security forces were deployed to protect the slip gate as the main artery for trade while Medina was without a voice in the stellar community."

"Well, that puts an end to that," said Rikeman with a grin. "Couldn't happen to a nicer bunch, but now that their whole blockade has failed, they'll no doubt be rushing back to push our salvager friends out again."

"That's a good thing, isn't it, sir?" asked Mia. "I mean, it means they'll need our protection more than ever, right?"

"More like it means Desert Rose will need to take what it can and get out while the getting's good," said Rikeman. "Even if we could entrench these dunes properly, we'd be badly outgunned when SanMontos brings back the bulk of its muscle. We're good, but they'd need twelve times our crew to go toe-to-toe with the cartels or the trade unions. I give it a week before they call our business concluded. They'll have made more from this expedition than they could have dreamed of by then anyway."

"And it's not like they'll be done with this site even then," commented Valerie, raising her mug with a smile. "With information of a find like this to broker, they may even be able to sign on with one of the bigger groups. I overheard talk that they might be able to strike a deal with Mother-Load, the salvage conglomerate, which *could* go toe-to-toe with the cartel. That alone could turn them into major competition. All in all, this was a jackpot operation for them, and not a bad one for our crew either."

"No. Not bad at all," said Rikeman. "In a few months, they may call us back to help them assault this site all over again with a few hundred other mech pilots and soldiers of fortune. I could definitely live with that."

Mia was distracted by the material playing across the screen. Among several replaying videos was a red blur that she recognized all too well. It was the *Anawim,* Electra and Aster's trademark ship, flying between frigates in the enormous blockade. The news stated openly, "Additionally, a mysterious ship entered the blockade, halting the entire SanMontos fleet. Some ships from within the blockade remain adrift with no explanation. Efforts continue to return the cruisers to normal operation. The Global Union denies knowledge of any vessel in Medinan space, but there is no record of the unmarked corvette.

Not only did President Ghuli deny the ship was of Global Union origins, but when questioned about the ship and whether it was related to the method of arrival, President Ghuli declined to comment, stating that he had sent for a Global Union fleet and not a single ship to break up the blockade after his arrival. This leaves many wondering as to the origins of this ship, its role and authority breaking past the SanMontos blockade, and its potential use in the GU President's sudden arrival at the summit meeting."

Mia shook her head with a smile. No doubt, Philos had intervened on Medina's behalf in some way yet to be revealed, and she suspected Electra and Aster and their ship had been involved.

A day later, the salvagers confirmed Jack's prediction. A fragment of the SanMontos ships had dispersed from the main fleet and were confirmed to be en route. However, it was also assessed that the local chapter had expended the majority of their combat resources in the last engagement and couldn't put up more than a token resistance now. This gave the Desert Rose salvagers an estimated eight days to plunder the underground bunker. Convoys transporting goods back to New McMurdo could ramp up for a time, and apart from a so-called "mild" sandstorm slowing their progress for a day, they did.

Mia's role as a scout was now obsolete. With only menial tasks, she was likely to be among the first ones cycled out, which she was fine with, as it left her free to plan a side trip she'd been meaning to make since she'd joined. The news of what happened on Medina may have left her no closer to discerning the nature of Electra and Aster's connection to Philos, but it was a place to start, and Mia hoped her friend would be the ideal person to consult about it.

As she packed to head out with the next load of goods, a notification interrupted the crew that a pay installment had been distributed from the operation. Mia's tail betrayed her astonishment as she saw the figure.

Nikki set a reassuring hand on Mia's shoulder and muttered, "Yeah, it's nice getting paid bucket loads of cash. Almost makes putting your life on the line worth it."

"I think I just made more in three weeks than I've collectively made in my life!" exclaimed Mia under her breath.

"Lemme see!" said Lynlee, curious.

"That's rude, you know," admonished Nikki.

"Says the one who's already peeked," fired back Lynlee.

"I didn't expect her to actually *show* me, okay?" said Nikki, then turned to Mia. "But relax. I'd say you earned that figure, given your contribution. So, do you have plans to celebrate?"

"I'm nervous enough about *having* this much money! Tempting as it sounds, I'm realizing that I've got a few things to do before I party like I'm at a rave station on Saturday night," Mia stated.

"But you have a destination in mind," said Nikki with a smirk.

"Midgard," murmured Mia. "Rikeman wants me to drop by Kiito station again to get my space suit and then meet up again later. I have a friend I haven't seen in years who lives there, so I'm angling to head out a day or so ahead of you. Eli volunteered to fly me out to Kiito ahead of time so I could spend a day on Midgard before we reconvene on the *John Henry*. Rikeman said it's not really practical to drag Tyber along for a side trip like this. It's not like we can buy a ticket and have him fly commercial, although I'm worried about leaving him to make the trip alone."

"I'll manage, m'lady," said Tyber. "These commercials sound uncomfortable anyway."

"That's true," said Nikki, stifling a laugh at Tyber's comment, "and if Jack lands the next contract he's set his eyes on, we'll all be meeting up at Midgard Orbital Station. Would that I could plan my downtime so well! I'll be lucky if I don't spend half of mine vacuuming the sand out of *Silver*!"

"You got it, although admittedly I didn't think of my friend Katelyn until Lynlee mentioned Midgard to me," said Mia. "It may be for the best that I go by myself, though. Much as I'd like to take Tyber along, I fear Katelyn will freak out if she sees him. Lynlee and Valerie have agreed to keep an eye on him until the *John Henry* arrives to pick everyone up. Now, you'll be sure to feed Tyber tonight and again while the *John Henry* is journeying from here to Midgard, right, Lynlee?"

"And blow-dry his fur after I brush the sand out, and cart out his poop when the *John Henry* unloads the fecal matter. You know, his schedule isn't all that different from ours, and he can remind me if I forget anything," stated Lynlee flatly. "So what does this Katelyn friend of yours do?"

"She's a data hoarder who makes her living in infor-mation exchange. You'd like her," said Mia with a gentle smile as she stood up with her bag. "I'll introduce you sometime if we get the chance."

At that moment, Eli stepped in the entryway with a travel pack of his own.

"Is that all you're bringing?" he asked.

"Yeah. I'm having the rest sent back to the *John Henry* for while I'm gone. Why?" asked Mia.

"I'm your ride to Kiito for your space suit," explained the technician with a friendly salute.

"I see. Rikeman did tell me to pack light," said Mia, intrigued, "but what are you planning to take us in? The *John Henry* isn't due back for a while, and it has all the freight shuttles."

"Captain Stratweiss left one of the *John Henry*'s escort craft back in New McMurdo for maintenance. I had my own reasons for dropping by Kiito, but when Rikeman heard I was willing to take you to Midgard, he pulled some strings to let me use it. It's a two-seater, and since you plan to pack light, we should be able to take you there without a hitch."

Mia was able to read between the lines. Eli was arranging an opportunity to speak privately, and by the sounds of it, he had gone to considerable lengths to do so. Mia had been pondering a way to get Eli to herself and ask him what he knew about Aster. His comment about her wrist display had not been forgotten, and she still wanted an explanation.

"All right. How soon can we go?" said Mia.

"The next convoy headed south is about to go if you're ready," replied Eli.

"I am," Mia said, then checked her bags and slung them over her shoulder.

"Then we'd better make sure they aren't kept waiting."

Having to keep her peace until they arrived in New McMurdo only served to make Mia giddy, particularly since traveling in the packed convoy vehicles was slower than their trip out had been. When they disembarked, Mia found herself asking, "So are two-man ships typical?"

"Not really, but this is one of our more adaptive strike craft. It has folding wings to optimize atmospheric flight. I'm actually rather fond of this model, even if I have more experience with IMP craft," said Eli.

"So do you mind explaining how you—" Mia started, but Eli seemed to know what she was going to ask and cut her off before she could finish.

"Hold that thought till we're in the pilot's cabin," said Eli, then lowered his voice. "The hangar carries sound so well, the walls might as well have ears."

Mia hesitated, feeling she'd already checked sufficiently that they were alone. Still, she had no desire to be overheard either, so she answered with a short but civil "Fine" and fought to contain herself as she followed the cryptic technician into the hangar.

From the outside, the spacecraft looked used but in fine condition, sitting at the ready with its wings retracted to minimize space. Eli did a thorough walk-around before opening the canopy and inviting her to take her seat. The inside was small, but between it and the tiny compartment for their belongings, it had just enough room to feel snug but not cramped.

"Okay, spill it! How do you know Aster?" Mia blurted out the instant they'd closed the canopy. "Not just anyone can recognize who my opssistant is meant to resemble."

Eli paused in his preflight check. He glanced back at her as she pointed to her wrist display, then, coyly looking at it, said, "What do you think, Aster? Are we safe enough from prying ears here?"

Mia looked down at her wrist display, where the opssistant appeared. It made like it was glancing about before giving a shrug and a nod.

Eli stared ahead for a time before he resumed preparing for takeoff. "Yes, I know Aster. However, I'd have an easier time giving you a full answer if you'd first share how you know the man who goes by Samuel Wilson. He's almost certainly your connection with them, and given the story circulating about your escape from the nomad megaship . . ." Eli trailed off, as if gathering his own thoughts, then asked, "Were Electra and Aster behind your escape?"

"Yes. That now makes two, no, three names you need to explain now," said Mia hotly, feeling she'd quite exhausted her patience.

"Be fair. It's hard to know one without the others," replied Eli. "Are they well? It's been years since I've seen either of them."

Mia felt defensive, but after taking a moment to calm herself, she replied with a deep breath. "They are. Frankly, I miss them. I'd shave my head for a picture of Electra with that carefree smile of hers. How long have you known? Was it when you saw my wrist display?"

"Wilson arriving with a new face was enough to make me guarded, but I admit the opssistant did help me put the rest of it together. You say they're well. Maybe I'm misreading you on this, but you seem worried for them."

"It's . . . complicated," said Mia. "Maybe it's more accurate to say I'm . . . concerned. I owe them so much. I wouldn't be here if it hadn't been for them, and they had no reason to help me. When I learned they were tied to Philos, I hit the ceiling. If Electra hadn't talked me down, I don't know what I would have done. I have a mountain of disjointed information that I can't identify, verify, or sort, and they are at the heart of it. What I do know is that 'Samuel Wilson' person has some kind of hold over them that binds them to Philos. I don't like it."

"Well, it's comforting to know they're still up to their old habits," said Eli. He then motioned for silence as he requested clearance to launch. The hangar doors opened, and the spacecraft departed in clockwork fashion. He adjusted their heading slightly before he turned and continued. "For what it's worth, I wasn't trying to evade your inquiries earlier. I haven't had the chance to talk with anyone about those two in a while. Of course, the last time I got to see either of them was when Aster helped me out of a tough scrape of my own. I was only nine then."

"Nine?" asked Mia in disbelief. Her eyes searched the air. "But that means she's been in that tiny body for . . . over a decade! Why would she do that to herself?"

"So she hasn't changed her look," said Eli, glancing back at her. "I thought so. I remember being shocked when I learned she wasn't my age back then too.

I suspect the only way we'll ever find out is if we ask her ourselves. All I know for sure is that pair has been around a lot longer than they let on."

"Probably even longer than that, given they don't have all their memories," said Mia in reflection.

"You know about their incomplete memories too?" asked Eli with a twinge of surprise. "Sounds like you three must have been very close then. Even I had to learn that secondhand. I'll bet you even know Samuel's callsign."

"He told me to use a specific name if I needed to ask for his help," said Mia tactfully. "Was he the one who told you about their loss of memory?"

Eli shook his head and replied, "Not in this case. More like I learned about it through one of our mutual acquaintances. Samuel Wilson isn't one to let things slip easily, although he likes to give you the opposite impression. Jack calls him 'Steve' just to stress that he knows 'Samuel' isn't his real name. That said, neither he nor Captain Stratweiss are aware of his Philos callsign, Xenos. My understanding is that's a name he generally only entrusts to people in Philos or people who have ties to his distant past."

"That can't be his real name, though," said Mia.

"I concur, just as I doubt 'Electra' and 'Asterope' are *their* real names either. The difference being that Xenos probably still knows his real name," said Eli. "Yet he's only ever opted to retain his callsign. He's a Philos go-between for Electra and Asterope, and he in turn has others who keep an eye on him."

"You mean like Philosophia?" asked Mia.

"Exactly," said Eli. "I suppose now it's my turn to share. I only know this secondhand, but the callsign 'Xenos' goes back as far as Philosophia itself. He was there when it was created, and it's fair to say he knows it better than anyone on this side of the dirt. That's why I suspect our meeting was arranged."

"Arranged? As in, he wanted you and me to meet and collaborate?" asked Mia.

"Meet, yes. Collaborate, maybe," said Eli. "The man is hard to predict, and just because I know *about* Xenos doesn't mean I actually *know* him. What I do know is that he's a man with his hand on the heartbeat of Philosophia, the most powerful AI mankind has."

"Or the reverse," said Mia. "Back on *Megalodon*, there were always theories that Philosophia was the one calling the shots for Philos and its major figures. The theory was it could think too far ahead of its programmers to be truly 'reprogrammed.' Talk about the stuff of nightmares!"

"I know, right?" said Eli. "If it isn't enough to make someone nervous, it's because they haven't been paying attention."

"Still, I'm glad I got to compare notes with you," said Mia. "I won't claim I knew how far back Xenos went before this, but I guess you could say I *sensed* it when I first saw him. It even makes sense, given the nature of artificial longevity. I wonder if Electra and Aster go back as far as he does. Still, what would Xenos gain by orchestrating our meeting?"

"*That* is a very good question," said Eli. "Sadly, I don't expect it is a question we will soon get an answer to. Perhaps he wanted you to understand how far his influence stretches or to caution you somehow. Or perhaps he simply knew I'd be able to relate as someone who's also brushed paths with his favorite operatives. For better or worse, we're both pieces in this game, and it's a game with more intrigue than I care for."

CHAPTER 17

New Context

Eli and Mia flew in silence for a time, preoccupied with their own thoughts as they set a course for the slip gate. A ship-mounted slip drive alone could enable most craft to traverse between planets orbiting the same star, but interstellar travel necessitated a slip gate, which enabled far greater distances to be shortened than any starship could achieve alone, and for small craft like theirs, riding aboard carrier ships to traverse the gate slipstreams was by far the safest method to ride by.

For a time, Mia occupied herself with her display, feeling she could explore it freely since Eli already knew of her connection to Electra and Asterope. Perhaps Aster had hidden something in the opsisstant program that Xenos might have overlooked. Some clue she might have wanted only Mia to see. Sadly, it seemed that if such a secret was enclosed in her link, it had yet to reveal itself, for she discovered nothing of consequence. The conversation with Eli had prompted Mia to examine her own motivations for investigating Electra and Aster's connections to Xenos, Philos, and the AI.

Perhaps Xenos's warning before their parting that they might never see each other again had been what bothered her most. She hadn't liked it, and neither had Electra or Aster, and yet they'd seemed compelled not to push the matter. Mia knew she wanted to visit her friends again, but more than that, she wanted it to be on their terms, not somebody else's. To do that, she had to better understand what kept them so tightly bound to Xenos of Philos.

Landing in Kiito was uneventful, and it was neat to see the new base's facilities as they took the chance to stretch their legs. Eli and Mia took their time, talking idly, taking an indirect route by way of several places on their way to the familiar shop. Mia's first mission on Zengin had been instructive, but she'd had surprisingly little interaction with much of the crew and knew only a few people outside those who made up the women's bunkroom. Hearing Eli's anecdotes about other members served to help her place several shipmates she'd only seen but not spoken with. They entered to find Tim examining a projected image of Tyber, writing down measurements, most notably around the head.

"Looks like Valerie sent you more than just *my* sizing," commented Mia.

"Yes. She told me in her last correspondence that you had hopes of building environmental gear for this big fellow. I was measuring to see what you might need to make him a breather system."

"Wait, you think you'd be able to do that?" exclaimed Mia. "I mean, I'd been meaning to ask someone like you who might be qualified for an odd job like this, but—"

"Oh, it's not as hard as you'd think," said Tim, a twinge of pride creeping into his voice. "I may need to learn more of Tyber's oxygen demands and lung capacity, but that's not too hard to fine-tune since breathing needs vary for everyone. Honestly, while a zoologist could give you some useful guidelines, *you* should be the one spearheading this operation as his trainer! With our fingertip access to data and ability to fabricate parts on demand, anyone passionate, willing, and thorough enough can achieve an expert's results. I'll give you the model I sketched out here and some of the more specialized parts to let you get started. If you like, I'm even game to take on a commission for something more robust later, provided you two are willing to send me the proper feedback, of course. Now, give me just a moment, and I'll go retrieve your new suit."

Tim disappeared into a back room and reappeared with Mia's space suit and pointed her to a place where she could discreetly change into it. Donning it was child's play, although Mia had to stifle a yelp of surprise when she pressed the button that made it constrict to her form. When she stepped out, Tim asked her to walk around in it to see how comfortable it felt while they talked.

"So will you be using your suit in the field for your next assignment?" Tim asked as Mia did some experimental stretches.

"Not in this case," said Mia. "If memory serves, Midgard is pretty breathable. I'm afraid I don't know enough about our next job to say anything about it either."

"Well?" asked Tim, turning to Eli as if the technician knew more than he was telling.

Eli rolled his eyes and replied, "If we land the job Rikeman's looking at on Gaia Volantis, we'll probably be sticking expressly to breathing masks, so probably not."

"Then why the rush for this suit?" asked Tim. "Normally, Rikeman gives new recruits a few missions to decide if they're a fit for the crew before he gets me involved."

Mia's face turned red, and she fumbled for something to say, as she had no wish to explain the unique circumstances that likely influenced Rikeman's decision to take her on as crew. Yet before she could speak, Eli smoothly interrupted.

"Oh, Mia's definitely a fellow Rail Driver at this point. She more than proved her quality on this last mission," said Eli with an affirming nod.

Mia blushed, feeling her cheeks burn at the praise.

"Gaia Volantis," repeated Tim with a nod. "Well then, I wish you two luck. I don't know all the details, but I seem to recall Gaia is a relatively ungoverned system neighboring some considerable political tension. I hope Rivkah is taking precautions."

"We're going out in a hearty convoy, with an ample starfighter escort for most of the journey," said Eli.

"Has she finally seen sense and armed another IMP craft in the launch bay for *you*?" asked Tim.

"My primary employment is with the Rail Drivers. A ship that can only *sometimes* be manned for escort isn't practical for the captain. Her offer still stands, though: If I can get an IMP craft of my own for the job, she'll pay me a full retainer and give me a good rate on hangar space. But that's still a ways off. That hardware isn't exactly cheap, you know."

"Well, that's reassuring at least. You'd be better off borrowing one if she were only offering you a technician's rates. Putting your own hardware on the line justifies a bit more than the cost to house it, after all," said Tim.

The two were moving across topics quickly again. Mia was simply glad she knew what they were referring to this time. The acronym IMP stood for "interchangeable mount platform," and it was a class of short-range spacecraft designed for zero-gravity navigation. Often called "imps," they were quite possibly the most common type of space-worthy craft in existence. *Megalodon* housed countless imps for maintaining its exterior systems, and almost every ship large enough to carry an IMP had at least one on board for maintenance, repairs, and the odd loading and unloading of cargo in orbit, like forklifts in a warehouse. Eli and Mia had even passed by several fitted with mining gear as they'd landed on Kiito, and Tim appeared to be servicing a brace in his workshop. IMPs were also widely used by pirates, since they could hold weapon mounts as well as tools to adapt them to a range of roles in plundering waylaid ships.

"Why am I only learning this about you now?" Mia asked with a sideways glance at Eli. "It sounds to me like you are more than just a *proficient* space pilot; you are an *exceptional* one."

"He's a fourth generation zero-G pilot. He's been flying imps from his parents' laps since he could walk," said Tim. "However, Eli's got sense enough not to brag. Flying escort can be one of the riskier ventures for a pilot."

After Tim gave Mia a few moments to confirm she was comfy in the suit, and had her don the helmet to examine the neckline's seal, he pressed his thumb to her shoulder like an artist checking his perspective, and nodded in approval.

"So is that it? Or is there something else I'm supposed to do?" asked Mia from inside her helmet.

"What you should do is take it for a spin before we go," said Eli. "I'll get my helmet and we'll take a brief stroll outside."

Not long after, the two of them stood at a nearby airlock, where Eli familiarized Mia with the suit's controls, then had her verbally walk him back through the procedures to demonstrate she knew her space suit protocol. As the outer airlock doors opened and they walked out, Mia looked about, surprised by the ease of movement.

"Except for the quiet, you almost forget you're in outer space," commented Mia, "I could get used to this."

"Nothing clears the mind like a space walk. So I take it you feel comfortable in your new suit?" asked Eli, turning over in a spaceborne summersault to glance back at her as he floated upside down over the walkway.

Mia nodded and replied, "I do."

"Excellent. Then I have one more thing to show you," said Eli as he rolled again and planted himself back on the ground. He turned and beckoned her closer. As Mia came near, Eli shut off his comms, then motioned for her to do the same. As she switched it off, Eli leaned in close and gripped her helmet so that it touched with his own.

"Can you hear me?" he said.

"I can," affirmed Mia.

"This is an old trick you can use if your comm system is down for whatever reason," said Eli, their touching helmets transferring sound between them. "It's also a fairly good way to talk in privacy. If in the future you ever need to share something with me in confidence, just ask me if you can join me on a space walk and snap off your comms system. I'll know what to do then."

"You'd had a trip like this planned from the moment you saw my wrist display, didn't you?" said Mia. "I guess I shouldn't have been such a pain about getting you to open up about Electra and Aster. You really take your privacy seriously, don't you?"

"Mia, you're trying to peek at the little man behind the curtain. The organization that controls the flow of information across multiple starfaring nations. However minute you think your goal may be in the grand scheme of things, I urge you to secure whatever privacy you can before you draw its attention," said Eli, then added with a hint of embarrassment, "Still, I hope you don't see me as paranoid."

"Miriam," said Mia suddenly.

"Pardon?" asked Eli.

"My actual name is Mi—" She stopped to make sure she said it the way she'd meant to. "Miriam. Electra and Aster filtered the data back to me about a day after we landed on Zengin III, along with some of Tyber's augmentation records. Even with practice, I still can't seem to say it consistently. I've been hesitant to tell anyone, since I'd have to explain why I wasn't going by that name from the get-go. But since you already know the reasons, I see no harm in sharing it with you."

"Miriam," repeated Eli. "That's a pretty name."

Glossary

Altaire Republic: Originally a republic, Altaire leads as one of the most powerful and prosperous interstellar nations. However, its cutting-edge technology has since caused many to wonder if the superpower should be reclassified as a technocracy. This is due to Philosophia: a powerful AI at the core of the Philos corporation, whose network operates to guide, if not govern and oversee, many aspects of Altaire logistics and daily life.

Augment: A generic term for someone utilizing cybernetics to augment their performance or interaction in some way. This can be anything as simple as neural implants to medical implants and artificial organs and memory systems, which in some cases can enhance bodily performance. (distinct from "posthuman")

Armsuit: Short for "exobionic armored suit," the term refers to an exoskeletal frame that can enhance a wearer's movements and mobility with a combination of artificial muscle fibers and hydraulics.

Crypto: The term for a basic unit of cryptographic currency, it tends to be stored on data cartridges and chips.

Cyborg: (see "Posthuman")

Data hoarder: A slang term for someone who backs up data they browse and find on online networks out of a fear it will be dismantled or lost in the ever-changing flow of information. This can be anything from videos and old media to virtual reality web pages duplicated from the ether of the Philos Network.

Desert Rose: A smaller salvage company, based out of Zengin III, that makes its money recovering machinery and resources from Zengin III's wastelands.

Eagle mod: A slang term for something so amazing it can't be legal to do or have. The term was coined by colonists railing against Earth gov regulations as "'egal modied," as a shortening of the term "illegally modi-fied," and the term further devolved with subsequent generations into "eagle mod."

FIVR: An acronym for "full immersion virtual reality," referring to systems that use neural implants to interface with software. Sometimes called "fiver play," it derives this name in part because the interface extends the user experience across all five senses.

Global Union: Though interstellar nations and cul-tures originally expanded like a fairy circle with an ever-increasing distance from Earth to limit its control over them, there came a time after Earth went silent that colonial powers expanded until they once more bumped into each other, creating friction and differences. With minimal ties to Earth left, the space fleets of Earth decided to reorganize their forces toward more constructive ends: namely an international agency dedicated to the universal preservation of peace and justice across all colonial nations. Whether it upholds these sublime ideals is a topic for debate, and colonies remain wary of the GU of this controversial agency.

H-cell: Short for "hydrogen cell"; H-cells are the standard form of energy cell to replace lithium-ion and lead-acid batteries after the hydrogen revolution of 2088, when it became apparent hydrogen could act as a storage medium for any form of generated power as efficiently and safely as existing batteries and fuels and posed almost no significant environmental impact compared to existing technologies.

Hypermagnetic rail mass driver: Sometimes called by simpler names like "mass driver," "rail driver," "railgun," and "HRMD," the hypermagnetic rail mass driver is a fancy term for a weapon that uses magnetism to fire projectiles at extraordinary speeds.

Mass driver: (see "Hypermagnetic rail mass driver")

Mechs: Terms for human-driven machines, as opposed to armsuits, which are human-worn armored exoskeletons. Mechs are an old dream many years in the making. Once too complex to design, much less merit their construction cost, advanced fabrication enabled the technology to be used in limited capacities, and its primary use has been as a military workhorse for frontline and hazardous work. Due to driver limitations, most mechs stand no more than fifteen feet tall. Often described as "tanks with arms and legs" they are often deployed as ARVs (armor recovery vehicles) and heavy sapping tools.

Megalodon: Originally fashioned as a deep-space colony ship, Megalodon is a ship of space nomads, people who, for various reasons, chose to forgo colonization in favor of general travel between existing colonies. Seeking to cut through the boundaries of civilization, it adopted the title "the city ship without borders" to illustrate its way of thinking. Now heavily modified from its original form, this megaship acts as a mobile space station for countless space nomads as it wanders through several star-faring nations in a general circuit, like a migrating bird with the seasons.

Megaship: A broad-ranging term for a large-scale starfaring ship. Often miles long in length, its utility varies from mass transport to colonization. Due to its sheer size, such ships tend to work with smaller vessels for mutual protection and are restricted in how close they can get to planetary bodies. "Megaship fleets" typically refer to a megaship and its associated escorts, since their sheer size tends to make them central hubs and mobile space stations in their own right, often meriting supply runs from smaller ships to stay sustained.

Mass Driver: (see "Hypermagnetic rail mass driver")

Mother-Load: A larger-scale salvage and shipping company based out of Zengin III.

Net diving: The use of virtual reality interfaces to explore internet pages and websites. While some sensational experiences, such as smell, touch, and taste, require the use of a neural implant to interface directly with the brain, many users settle for use of virtual reality gear in the form of headsets, contacts, or kinetic feedback gloves to engage online through this platform.

Philos: The corporate body that supports much of the Philos Network, through which it offers its artificial intelligence services via their AI, called Philosophia.

Philos Network: A vast online network of server systems spanning dozens of worlds and linked using quantum entanglement transceivers to facilitate faster-than-light communication across space. While not quite the same as the internet, the Philos Network stands as the largest single system of information networking in place, and what few information platforms don't fall under its domain are still heavily influenced by its presence.

Philosophia: Currently mankind's most sophisticated AI, Philosophia has existed for generations as an information entity with widespread influence across multiple star-faring nations.

Posthuman: The trending term for a human cyborg who has, for one reason or another, converted enough of their mind and/or body to cybernetics to achieve a state of artificial longevity. Considered a soft-definition for someone who doesn't have an organic body, its meaning is almost deliberately ambiguous.

Raiden Alliance: The title of a band of freedom fighters who splintered from the Singularity Dawn and have risen to gain exceptional notoriety. An insurrection conceived with the support of the Altaire Republic, the Raiden Alliance has funded much of its campaign through private backing and mercenary work for other factions, exchanging favors with the interstellar kleptocracy's many mutual enemies to protect their dream of liberation.

Rail gun: (see "Hypermagnetic rail mass driver")

Rave station: Designed to skirt the boundaries of planetary jurisdiction, a rave station is a slang term for a hastily built space station that is usually deposited in a distant orbit around a planet to facilitate wild parties.

Reál: The standard unit of physical currency favored most by spacefarers. Based expressly on material value, its monetary value directly correlates to market prices by using fixed measures and on-demand fabrication.

SanMontos Cartel: A megacorporation specialized to terraforming infrastructure and colony supplies, including food, clothes, tools, parts, and vehicles.

Singularity Dawn: A powerful oligarchic kleptocracy and current rival to the Altaire Republic, it is renowned for its iron rule through a centrally managed economy and society, utilizing technology and fear to coerce its people into cooperation.

Slip drive: Short for "inertial slip drive," this method of travel is what most ships use to traverse between planets by harnessing the power to bend and compress space around a ship to move around, multiplying the vectors of objects in motion. The warped area tends to be called "slip space" or a "slipstream."

Slip gate: A type of node generally positioned in key positions in or near star systems, these conduits warp space between them to reduce the distance between stars, creating a "slipstream" that ships can travel along to move between stars. It further reduces the travel time between stars the way standard slip drive reduces the time and energy needed to travel between planets.

Space nomad: While applicable to most any starfarer who makes their home among the stars, the term tends to be applied to a person who makes their home on one of the megaship fleets that wander between worlds without settling in any permanent sense. Often culturally compared to gypsies, they tend to have a mixed reputation as free spirits who in some cases specialize in the clandestine, if not illegal.

Trade unions: A generic term for commercial conglomerates predating most of the colony nations, they are among the establishments that dominated commercial space before Philosophian logistics. Initially, they fought Philos and the transhumanist movement, but its odd tendency to look out for their ability to do business freely has since put them in a more neutral standing with the tech giant.

Quantum entanglement transceivers: A transceiver that uses the principles of quantum entanglement and "spooky action at a distance," as Einstein famously called it, to transmit large amounts of data. These linked particles can transmit instantly over any distance, but only to each other. It is the only form of faster-than-light communication available short of the utilization of slip-drive couriers to physically carry data between colonies. Because of the intensive building constraints involved, these transmitter dyads are extremely rare, and most colonies seldom have more than one tightly monitored set with which to network with the inter-stellar community.

Character List

(in order of appearance)

Mia: Space nomad and main character of our story. Mia, as most call her, is, genetically speaking, human, although her mannerisms match her biographed ears and tail to the point where it would cause one to wonder, and she doesn't like to talk about it.

Tyber: The name of a military-grade tiger genetibeast with artificially induced sapience. A seemingly fluke result of a process that seldom yields notable intellect among creatures, Tyber's "uplifted" intellect poses a plethora of ethical dilemmas and puts him in a somewhat precarious state. Aware but undaunted by this, he has chosen to set out with Mia to explore the world and see it for himself.

Callsign "Electra": A callsign given to the kindhearted and powerful posthuman who works in espionage in conjunction with Philos. While capable of many appearances, she defaults to a look with long chestnut-brown hair and elegant, form-fitting garb. Yet this belies her ability to use her cybernetically augmented body, which gives her seemingly superhuman levels of strength and speed.

Callsign "Asterope": Smaller than her counterpart, callsign Asterope (or Aster, for short) is acclimated toward machine and computer interface. While some of her methods remain shrouded in mystery, what is known is she boasts some of the most adaptive and powerful hacking techniques and programs ever seen, testifying to the sheer intellect hiding behind this child's silvery eyes.

Callsign "Xénos": More widely known as Samuel Wilson, this callsign belongs to a mysterious accountant and resource analyst of Philos whose close association with Electra and Aster remains a point of mystery.

Rho (Ρ ρ): (Called Rhonda for day-to-day interactions.) The designation of a Philosophian android "aspect" assistant attached to Samuel Wilson who serves as his aid. Often dressed in professional garb, the android is designed to assist and protect the auditor with professionalism and poise while drawing as little attention as possible.

Elias Lambert: (Often called Lambert and Lambi despite his dislike of the names). Technician for the Rail Drivers who is often floated between the mercenary company and the crew of the freighter, the *John Henry*, for his skills repairing and operating machinery.

Captain James "Jack" Rikeman: A rugged veteran from Caladria with a powerful build and a golden horseshoe mustache. He established the Rail Driver Mercenary Company and leads them as their captain.

Lynlee: An upbeat, ebullient teenage technician, she stands as one of the Rail Drivers' younger members. She works hard to support their operations with her technical acumen and bright smile.

Valerie Garnier: Although only a med tech, Valerie is presently assistant head physician for the Rail Drivers and the *John Henry*. Despite being less qualified than her superior, she does the majority of the footwork aboard the ship on behalf of Dr. Roche, the official head physician, coordinating paramedic teams.

Darek Carter: Chief of Security for Kiito mining base. He is a long-term acquaintance of Jack Rikeman and seems quite familiar with the Rail Driver Mercenary Company.

Nikki Li: A passionate, strong-willed mech pilot who dresses in a black jacket and a red jumpsuit to match her mecha (lovingly named Silver). She loans out her skills to the Rail Driver Mercenaries in exchange for the occasional favor as she strives to help the Raiden Alliance, a group of rebels trying to liberate their people from the oppressive Singularity Dawn.

Tim: The man who constructs the space suits for the Rail Driver Mercenaries. According to Rikeman and Eli, he used to do work as one of them before retiring to the role on Kiito Mining Base.

Captain Rivkah Stratweiss: The diminutive captain of the *USS John Henry*. She has worked her whole life in stellar shipping. She is often seen wearing an officer's hat and a ceremonial sword that almost drags the ground.

Sergeant 'Evski: A veteran rifleman and recon scout who earned his scars before joining the Rail Drivers, he's a tough rifleman whose tactical awareness, old school methods of fighting, sheer resilience, and mysterious past make him a local legend among the Rail Driver Mercenaries.